Tomorrow's
Alternatives

FRONTIERS 1

Tomorrow's Alternatives

ORIGINAL SCIENCE FICTION

edited by ROGER ELWOOD

COLLIER BOOKS
A Division of Macmillan Publishing Co., Inc.
NEW YORK

COLLIER MACMILLAN PUBLISHERS
LONDON

Macmillan Publishing Co., Inc.
866 Third Avenue, New York, N.Y. 10022
Collier-Macmillan Canada Ltd.

Frontiers 1: Tomorrow's Alternatives is also published in a hardcover edition by Macmillan Publishing Co., Inc.

Library of Congress Catalog Card Number: 73–6060

First Collier Books Edition 1973

SECOND PRINTING 1974

Printed in the United States of America

Preface

THE BEST ANTHOLOGIES are those that afford authors the opportunity to bring into being brand-new stories. Certainly for the compiler it is most stimulating to work on all-original anthologies—such as the present volume.

There are problems, to be sure: one quite well-known author has a habit of *not* making deadlines; another will not write a story unless it can have at least one pornographic scene in it. I *try* not to deal with such authors as the first; and I *never* deal with the second. (As far as I am concerned, science fiction that must depend upon sexual explicitness is built upon a pretty poor foundation.)

Compiling an anthology properly is an agonizing job; only you, the reader, can judge if this book is a good one. But, I assure you, it was put together slowly and carefully.

The authors represented herein are a "mix." Some are long-time professionals; others are newer authors; at least one is a complete beginner. But all have one thing in common: masterly storytelling abilities.

Stylistically, there is great diversity. The Silverberg approach, as indicated by "Ship-Sister, Star-Sister," is certainly much different from that of Clifford D. Simak's in "Univac: 2200." Stephen Goldin and C. F. Hensel have combined definite social commentary with bittersweet qualities; and "Mommy Loves Ya" by David H. Charney is a survival story with a tender thread running through it. Lafferty is *pure* Lafferty with "In Outraged Stone." And Malzberg is *pure* Malzberg with "Those Wonderful Years."

Gene Wolfe's story, "Peritonitis," is one of his best; "Getting Around" by K. M. O'Donnell is top-drawer (we hope you agree); Lee Saye's "Morning Rush" is both amusing and chilling; Terry Carr's "The Answer" seems a change of pace for this well-known author. And Richard Posner, one of the brightest of the newer authors, does a fine job with "Jacob's Bug," a story with a surprise ending that we don't think you will guess. Then Barrington Bayley comes on strong, showing he deserves his reputation, with "Mutation Planet."

You will probably find Frank Herbert's introduction to be far meatier than most; it offers some challenging thoughts about tomorrow's alternatives, and deserves to be read, and studied, as a separate and worthy work in its own right.

Just what does tomorrow hold? What are the alternatives to today? Will life improve? Or will it simply deteriorate to a level more nightmarish than any encountered today?

These stories tackle such questions, as well as others. Some are fanciful in their projections; others are deadly serious. All were written with an awareness of the fact that you, the modern science fiction reader, demand not bug-eyed monsters and invasions from space but stories that are thought provoking and meaningful.

A special debt of thanks to my editor, Fred Honig: a patient man, and someone whose views have been of tremendous service toward the compilation of a better book.

ROGER ELWOOD

Contents

Introduction:
Tomorrow's Alternatives?

FRANK HERBERT

A fable for our times (about half past tomorrow). If you believe you recognize in this fable any dolls living or dead, you could be suffering from a warped reality.

ONCE UPON A TIME there was a factory operated by dolls. The factory was called *Reality* and it was built in the land of *Possible* where improbable things often occurred. The factory manufactured guns and dolls, and it supposedly operated on a self-limiting principle. When there were too many dolls, the factory turned out more guns, which were intended to reduce the doll population.

An improbable thing happened, however. At the end of each supposedly self-limiting cycle, *Possible* found itself with more dolls *and* more guns than had existed before the start of the cycle.

This unexpected relationship between dolls and guns did not make itself immediately apparent to the factory's doll managers, who were a select group within the regular output of *Reality*. Even when some dolls began to suggest such a relationship, their speculations were made the object of laughter. Everyone knew *Reality* had been designed on a self-limiting loop of the Universal Continuum and that the factory's controls had been left in the hands of the dolls by the Original Builder.

It came to pass then that the dolls of *Possible* found *Reality* straining to its limits. The cycles turned faster and faster. The entire process developed odd wobbles and eccentricities. Parts of *Reality* often were attacked and sometimes damaged. The factory's managers took to shoring up their structure which, through long addition and revision, appeared rambling and haphazard. The repairs were sometimes makeshift and improbable. Everyone from the highest managerial circles to the lowliest laboring dolls felt beleaguered, the target of threats too large to be understood.

Possible's dolls began more and more to question self-limiting as a principle. Some sneered at doll control. Great blocs of dolls even openly denied that there had been an Original Builder. They substituted the Theory of the Grand Accident, sometimes called The Enormous Dichotomy.

All of this time, *Reality* seethed with questions about how to produce more guns and/or more dolls, or better dolls or better guns. Many splinter groups formed. Some argued for limiting guns, others for limiting dolls. An organizational schism developed within the factory. A large body of dolls revised an ancient concept called Deterrent Defense and named it now Sacred Security. Each splinter group developed its own factions. Many argued for such programs as speeding up the cycles or aiming for improbable goals of doll efficiency and gun efficiency. Gun to doll and doll to gun ratios were examined with fine attention to detail. Doll support and gun support became issues of the moment while the effects of such eccentric alternation reverberated throughout *Possible*.

A curious transformation began to occur in the dolls flowing from the factory. Some of the managers called it a manufacturing flaw and argued for new and better controls on doll production. Discontinuance of entire lines of dolls was proposed and some tried to carry out such programs, but the curious transformation continued. It assumed a major form called *Variants*. They were divided primarily into two categories: dolls intended for functions concerned mainly with doll quality and welfare began doing things which increased the production of guns; gun-oriented dolls began to deny the principles beneath their function. It frequently was difficult to tell a doll-doll from a gun-doll.

In all of *Possible* there now remained only a few small doll voices saying: "Let us re-examine the whole function of *Reality*. Perhaps we have been blinded to important parts of the system by our belief in improbable principles."

So few dolls paid attention to these warnings, however, that the mad cycles continued unabated—faster and faster, more and more eccentric. Finally, the whole system came crashing down in one last paroxysm of dolls and guns. *Reality* was left in ruins and *Possible*, stripped of all its dolls, reverted to a barren wilderness where chaotic improbabilities reigned supreme.

Moral: If you were built to prefer either dolls or guns, perhaps you were intended only for a limited function.

THE FUTURE THAT ISN'T

WHEN I was quite young, long before I became perfect (a perfected thing), I began to suspect there must be flaws in my sense of reality. It seemed to my dim sense of confusion that *things* often blended, one into another, and the Law of the Excluded Middle merely opened up a void wherein anything was possible. But I had been produced to focus on objects (things) and not on systems (processes). This left so much unexplained that no thing behaved invariably as intended, provided that such a concept as *intention* could be entertained even for an instant.

What was even more important, I had somehow acquired an obvious predilection for excluding myself from all considerations about the world around me. A *thing?* Me? How awful!

This led naturally to a belief that I could be the sole exception to any rule which I detected. Rules were made for things, not for me, possessor of absolute free will.

In some odd fashion, all of the fellow humans I encountered appeared to have this same belief. Not a one of them seemed to suspect that our universe might be larger, more complex and subtle than our presumptive little *Laws* assumed. I reasoned that an unspoken (or unrecognized) assumption might be a signpost at the outer limits of where we humans ventured, but this *personal exclusion principle* confused me. It made it difficult to question the authenticity of any *Law* because the arguments kept returning to things which needed "no further explanation" and which "everybody" knew.

Except me—I didn't know.

This did little more than make me feel stupid and force me into actions which were asinine, to say the least: either I agreed hypocritically that "sure, everybody knows that" or I just joined all the rest of my kind in refusing to examine such disturbing areas. After all, what were the assumption signposts set up for?

Thus, I was taught to believe utterly and unquestioningly in principles and even more so in First Principles, the ones from which there could be no exclusions (except me). It was a universe of absolutes which provided me with an infinite source of comforting reassurances. It said:

"All questions have answers."

However, with my core of confusion—an unprincipled attitude—I suspected a flaw in the fabric of the universe: a question, one at the very least, without any answer whatsoever.

Despite what my fellow humans, western variety, employed as consensus reality, my own set of local beliefs came to contain more and more naked kings. This was a series of very traumatic experiences.

The frustrations of these early traumas led me to formulate five assumptions for my own study of reality. Because I want many of the words which follow to be a shared exploration of possible futures (alternative realities) with emphasis on humankind's Utopian dreams, it seems only fair to begin the sharing with a brief statement of these assumptions.

Assumption I: There exists a kind of self-reflexive laugh reaction in humankind which often releases tensions and links us to that balance which we call sanity. (If I cannot laugh at myself, I risk turning the whole future and sanity business over to non-laughers.)

Assumption II: Many Academic/Scientific Futurists who supposedly are guiding our philosophic and technologic trip through Time have a monkey on their backs, a burden of memories and concepts which contain alternate, often mutually exclusive versions of reality. (A monkey on the back sometimes can be detected by its characteristic chattering.)

Assumption III: If we define Futurism as an exploration beyond accepted limits, then the nature of limiting systems becomes the first object of exploration. (Some people who say they are talking about a future are only talking about their own self-imposed limits.)

Assumption IV: A prominent and commonly accepted reality matrix by which Futurism and Reality are interpreted suffers from false assumptions about control. The false assumptions can be described thusly: that manipulation can be absolute, and that power is not subject to relativistic influences.

Assumption V: Implications of Relativity Theory have not been applied to the ways humans relate to each other or to the ways humans relate to the universe. (We tend to project the future onto a screen whose subtitle says: "It's better to live in a box than to face up to infinity.")

Five assumptions represent a weak arsenal with which to go up against thousands of years of reality production. It's one thing to recognize that consensus reality (our ideas about common belief) includes errors. It's quite another thing to put on Don Quixote's armor, take up the Lance of the Five Assumptions, and charge forth to do battle with a dystopic universe. Rebellion can make you just as drunk as pot or alcohol, and there's no guarantee that recognition of error will direct you to a proper correction of that error.

A city planner once told me his job was to seek "a compromise between the impossible and the improbable."

This aphorism tied off a long harangue in which he had detailed his frustrations over trying to prevent a housing development on a flood plain which had been taken over by real estate speculators.

I asked him if he had even once looked at the problem from the point of view of the speculators, whose assumptions and the context defined by those assumptions had led them into this "anti-social" behavior. He dismissed my question as "politically naive."

Our *scientific* culture, like the Victorian-industrial culture before it, sets sharp limits on what it will accept as a reality experience. Step outside those limits and the influence they have on the kinds of futures the society says it will permit, and you get cut off.

There's obvious fallacy in the concept that you can deal with any problem as an isolated bit all of whose consequences can be anticipated and "controlled." But consensus reality, reinforced by conformity, language and conditioning, continually traps us into positions where we deny that awareness by our actions.

My five assumptions tell me there are no facts, only observational postulates in an endlessly regenerative mish-mash of predictions—some faulty, some accurate . . . for the time being. To *plan for the future*, to attempt guiding humankind into "the better life" which our Utopian dreams define, we are involving ourselves with the monitoring and manipulation of *change*. This means inevitably that we change our frame of reference, our consensus reality.

But all around us exist societies demanding fixed frames of reference. In a multi-level universe, there can be no absolute fixed frames of reference and thus no absolute consensus reality. A relativistic universe makes it impossible to test the reliability of any expert by requiring him to agree with another expert. Both can be correct— within their individual frames of reference.

The city planner and the real estate speculator are both correct. Richard Nixon and the Students for a Democratic Society are correct—each in his own context. Mao and Nixon are both right.

Comes now the *Futurist* and the *Ecologist*, each with his bag of expertise, each making new demands and asking new questions. Comes now the SDS (and other "radicals") accusing: "You won't give us a better world because you're bad."

Each is *right* and each is *wrong*.

The five assumptions suggest to me that we are making many pointless demands and are asking many meaningless questions. We often do this after developing an "expertise" within a frame of reference which has little or no relationship to the frame of reference within which the questions are asked or the demands are made.

It is as pointless for the SDS to ask Nixon "Why are you so bad?" as it is for Nixon to demand of the SDS "Why are you so crazy?" Each bedazzled by his own *rightness* and the other's *wrongness* fails to see a larger system whose dynamics have us all resonating.

The dolls are jumping. They are performing in response to a multitude of system-influences, most of which are only dimly understood by the performers. Advice comes from all sides, each bundle of pronouncements translated from a specialized expertise (local reality) which sets the whole system bouncing, often in unexpected ways. The leaders of each frame of reference guide that framework as though it were the only exception to all of the rules they have discovered. It appears to be an odd amplification of the *personal exclusion principle*.

It would seem that a Futurist concerned with our Utopian dreams needs to listen, to observe and to develop expertise to fit the problems, not the other way around. But that is not our dominant approach.

Let us pause a moment and advance a tentative postulate based on my Assumption V (and the Special Theory of Relativity).

Postulate I: When taken out of a larger system of dynamic relationships, all inertial frames of reference are equivalent.

According to this postulate, both Pakistan and India are equally right, and equally wrong. The same applies to Democrats and Republicans, to Left and Right, to Israel and the Arab states, to Irish Protestants and Irish Catholics. The latter would appear in this view still to be resonating to the Battle of the Boyne with consequences no less bloody than those of the original.

This postulate says any group seeking to defend its own reality (frame of reference) at the expense of another group's reality will be led into a circular argument and inevitably will try to prove its own *rightness* in terms of faith expressed as propositions whose most basic assumption can be translated this way:

"I believe this because I want to believe it (or because it is so beautiful, or so simple, or so obvious, etc.)."

In this light, the advocacy principle behind western law/jurisprudence, insofar as it ignores the wild vibrations it may set up in larger systems, appears to suffer from a basic flaw.

From within the boundaries of any specialized viewpoint, these are outrageous statements. I can say to you they are based in part on mathematics (*we inevitably are led to prove any proposition in terms of unproven propositions*) or upon physics (*no absolute frame of reference can be demonstrated*). Neither statement subtracts from that first flush of outrage. Indeed, *Postulate I* leads inexorably to an even more outrageous postulate.

Postulate II: Logic that is sound for a finite system is not necessarily sound for an infinite system.

This asserts that no matter how tightly you construct a system of arguments and close up all of the holes in your globe of reality, an infinite universe predicts a larger system outside of yours which can negate everything you say.

There are no impenetrable boxes in an infinite universe.

I am saying to you that a Futurist, as the role is presently recognized, who functions on this planet in this universe, must act within the rigors of these postulates unless he can produce another frame of reference which demonstrates greater operational reliability.

At this point, I can involve myself blindly in the circular definition game. I can assemble arguments from philosophy (no man is an island), from psychology (all organisms are primarily motivated to control and modify their environment), from physics and mathematics (see above), etc. to defend my assumed wide-angle assault on accepted limiting frameworks. It should be obvious, however, that my assumptions and postulates already possess circular characteristics, are based on existing systems, and eventually go back to an unproven proposition which says:

"I believe this because I want to believe it."

What is it I believe?

I believe we are well into a period when technological developments exert greater and greater influence on the individual human life, often with shockingly destructive consequences.

I believe we are engaged in a crisis of the human species which is shared by all and that it is pointless to discuss Futurism or Utopian dreams without recognizing the nature of this crisis.

I believe the explosive core of this crisis involves an energy-release cycle which is running wild. I see the fate of the species inextricably tangled with the fate of the individual, if for no other reason than that the individual is becoming a releaser of greater and greater energy bundles.

Any number of my fellow humans have pointed to this

energy focus—the amount of energy one individual can release—and how this is increasing on an exponential curve which is climbing at a wild-growth rate.

When you consider the destructive energy represented in this curve, it gives you such comparisons as this: The murderers of Mary Stuart's husband, Darnley, had to fill a basement with explosives to assassinate the royal consort. Today, they could carry the equivalent energy in a rather small satchel. Furthermore, explosive materials are more readily available in our age. If I were insane enough to wish to destroy a building, murdering a head of state, I could do it with a device incorporating materials purchased from a corner drugstore.

The amount of energy available for misuse is increasing beyond the point where one person is able to wreck the planet we all share. We have no guarantees that such energy will remain in the hands of individuals who will not do this.

With human defined as "like me," I believe we suffer from a world sickness whose most destructive symptom is a denial of that likeness. This is an absurd sickness. It represents taking up arms against yourself in the name of taking up arms against others.

In the face of all this, I believe that humankind need not come to a cataclysmic end, that we can engage ourselves, as a species, with infinity. I am aware of the growth-cycle arguments against this viewpoint. ("All organisms, including societies and civilizations, go through a process of birth, maturation and death.") I hear the chorus of cynical "cannots." I am also aware that the statement "I cannot" often is an unconscious substitute for "I will not." I am saying to all such doomscriers: The man who turns against himself or against his fellowman —either singly or as part of a massive effort—is running away from life, is admitting a defeat which his own actions help create.

A kind of moral cowardice can be sensed in wanting to believe only what comforts us. Thus, I give you no absolute assurances behind any of these beliefs. Indeed, in the universe I am describing, we are destined forever to find ourselves shocked to wakefulness on paths we do not recognize, in places where we do not want to be, in a universe which does not care about our distress, which has no anthropomorphic center from which even to notice us.

A basic distress shared by all of humankind and against which we have raised so many fragile defenses—that death may cancel us out—comes with the original package and remains with it. Despite all of our efforts to project anthropomorphic images onto this universe, it continually presents us with a view of chaos. In this view, we breast a grey void which conceals our uncertain future, uncertain except for one thing: That which we perceive here disappears into the void, and we interpret that disappearance as an ending.

To much of humankind, this represents a vision of ultimate despair. In this desperate moment of our species, with extinction real and imminent, there grows a suspicion that we may occupy the only island of life which has ever occurred. Indeed, the statistical arguments for extraterrestrial life remain unproven and smell of ad hoc constructions, a kind of collective whistling past the cemetery. We want to believe these arguments because they comfort us in our moment of despair. (In this light, science fiction appears more akin to religion than to escapist entertainment.)

In the typical dichotomous trap, we are offered the alternatives of belief (one of the old "tried and true" beliefs or any of the new ones which proliferate around us) or participation in profound despair.

But why should any human (any *life*) remain confined in the arena of "either/or" when an infinite universe offers us its boundless playground? Who says we have only two choices? Another perception of *Infinity* says: "No cages or boxes—ever." What a joyful vision unfolds in this perception. Here appears a concept of *freedom* beyond any other dream.

How do we sensitize ourselves to such a *free* universe?

How do you examine a system of which you are a part? What unconscious blinders narrow the vision of our questions?

Try these for a multi-dimensional leverage:

Postulate III: Any dichotomy confronts us ultimately with contradictions. (Unless we are prepared to be taught by and then abandon contradictions, the "yes-or-no" arena represents a trap.)

Postulate IV: All answers represent mirror images of the questions which produced them. (If we ask a question from a "go/no-go" assumption, we get both "go" *and* "no go" answers. Both are inherent in the question and thus are inherent in the answers.)

Our questions tend to ignite awareness and to limit the kinds of answers we get. The *mirror* reflects a state of consciousness as well as the direction in which our attention is aimed.

These postulates indicate that a small bite may best be savored in terms of a whole meal. If I say to you that I am a transient visitor at an endless banquet, this can mean that I have heard an invitation and have accepted it. (The suggestions that more and more of humankind is hearing the invitation, but is unable to respond, has been advanced several times as a major element of the crisis in which the species finds itself.)

If we must be prepared to abandon answers to any question how do we rebuild our *Reality* factory and set it to producing operational frames of reference? Our aim could be defined this way: to develop ways of dealing with an infinite universe, ways which allow for non-lethal emergency changes of direction. The framework we're dealing with is the one upon which we hang our sense of reality. Remember that one of our preliminary requirements is that we not become explosively disoriented.

Here are a few questions just to begin our exercise in a multi-dimensional infinite universe. Try your own answers, being prepared to abandon any assumption (all answers provisional), noting limits and aims of any new questions which may be ignited in you by my questions and suggestions.

1) When frames of reference come into conflict, how do we compare and relate them while keeping survival avenues open for our species? (If we are mediating with methods which have always led to disasters in the past, why do we continue employing such methods?)

2) How do we distinguish between our technology, the world which influences it (and is influenced by it) and the universe outside this framework?

3) Do determinist concepts such as "progress" hide us from the terrors of an uncertain future while beguiling us with sugarplum visions which can visit us with bloody disasters?

4) How can we deal with lag times for out-of-date information, especially when such information represents power and identity to entrenched blocs of our fellow humans?

5) Does identifying a larger spectrum of influences upon myself and my fellows necessarily lead to a dampening of deadly resonances in our mutual system?

6) Isn't it odd that we've never mounted a full-scale investigation into whether pheromones (external hormones) interact between members of our species the way they interact within other animal species? (That $52 million spent last year in the United States for the purchase of vaginal deodorants does more than disturb my sense of reality.)

7) Is it enough to say "I am human and you are human," or is it closer to the mark to say "I am animal and you are animal"? (How about "I am alive and you are alive"?)

8) Is it possible to demand absolute answers from an infinite universe?

9) If we are to be suspicious of even the *processes* by

13 | TOMORROW'S ALTERNATIVES?

which we create our images of reality, where do we look for a stable horizon by which to keep our balance?

10) Is it sufficient to have each other, to be a world-band of humans in motion through a moving universe?

Enough of this question game.

The surfer, the swimmer and the skier should have a body-sense of what I am suggesting we require as a species-sense. Oddly enough, it also may help if you recall the last time you sat in a movie theater with your attention focused on the screen and its attendant sounds.

Jean Piaget, the famed co-director of the Institute of Educational Science in Geneva, Switzerland, sets the stage. Piaget, in *The Construction of Reality in the Child,* begins his discourse by stating flatly that "the budding intelligence constructs the external world." He says we not only furnish this composition with permanent objects in a spatial universe, but also construct "a world obeying the principle of causality," and that this stable external universe remains "distinct from the internal world."

He notes from his long observation and experimentation that the human develops an "object concept" which, "far from being innate or given ready-made in experience, is constructed little by little." Further, he observes that recognition of objects is "extended into belief in the permanence of the object itself."

Thank you, Doctor. But out of what does the budding intelligence construct its external world of causal relationships and permanent objects?

Somewhere between my twentieth and thirtieth years, I began to suspect I was on a railway trip, and instead of a conductor and engineer, my journey was under the direction of a movie projectionist. This projectionist with his little machine situated somewhere in my consciousness carried major influence over what I perceived as reality. If something disagreed with *projection-reality*, a filter dropped into place and I did not sense that disagreement. Nothing came through. But if something agreed with *projection-reality*, the spotlights came on, the music, the drama, the amplifiers. I became engrossed and all too willing to suspend my critical sense of disbelief.

Motion and illusion, that's all it was.

With this thought came a gigantic suspicion: Perhaps even the motion was unreal. Who needs motion when he has a projectionist as talented as this? There was no trip at all, no waystops, no terminals—just that projectionist throwing his illusions upon the colossal screen which was my sense of reality.

"We are such stuff as dreams are made on. . . ."

There can be only a jury-rigged ad hoc response to this solipsist giggling in all philosophers' nightmares. Instead of throwing up our hands in rage and fear, however, let us ask what this bit of solipsism tells us. What can we learn from the inevitable store of illusion always beyond our transient reality?

Postulate V: There are questions which can never be answered. (The mathematician demonstrates that there are problems which can never be solved.)

Watch out for the play of the verb *to be* in my words, in the work of mathematicians, of physicists and other scientists. Every now and then, a bit of something extraordinary shows through the illusory screen. The causal absolutes don't quite filter out everything which might disturb our fixed sense of reality. There are shadows, *ombres chinoises,* figures out of context. It's like an audience arriving late for the show, stepping on our toes and casting their shadows on our screen in spite of the busy projectionist.

When I said *nothing* came through the filtering system, I should have added *most of the time.*

To be carries a heavy load of Piaget's objective, fixed, causal absolutism into the "budding intelligence." That little indefinite article, *the,* aids mightily in this reality-building.

"*The* answer *is.* . . ." (Supply your own ending.)

I am not suggesting you immediately discard all forms of *to be* and that you substitute *a* for *the* from this point onward. Filters can be useful when you understand how they operate. No movie cameraman has to wait for moonlight to produce a moonlight effect. He can use a blue filter. Most audiences understand this. It's one of the conventions we accept in this art form.

You ask yourself now: Is he suggesting that the building of our consensus reality may be an *art form*? If so, what have we been experiencing, a theater of the macabre?

A look at the scenario for 1971 suggests something even worse than the macabre.

Ten Million Refugees Flee Pakistan
U.S. Escalates Air War in Southeast Asia
New Bomb Kills Every Living Thing Within 3,000 Feet
Belfast Bomb Kills Child
Napalm Survivors: A Legacy of the Maimed
Three Policemen Murdered
Palestinian Guerrillas Raid Village—10 Dead
Bangladesh Death Toll May Top Million
Israelis Level Arab Village
Prisoners Tortured to Death in Dacca
Starvation: Way of Life on American Indian Reservation

Who wrote this scenario?

You did. I did. Others among the 3.5 billion of our fellow humans on this ball of dirt did. Our ancestors contributed many of the lines. Some of the bits came from chaotic influences. Many oscillations can be identified as resonating through our species. We have influenced and been influenced. We have acted and been acted upon.

A physicist sees our universe as quantum-mechanical with energy locked in various frequency phenomena (and with energy available through manipulation of such phenomena). Human relationships can be seen as frequency phenomena. We have a wave nature.

There *is* a tide in the affairs of men.

We respond to wave-form influences; we perform strange dances to strange music. We occupy (and are occupied by) a multi-wave, multi-level system whose dynamics we do not understand. We interrelate with our system in transient ways, and the interlocked weight of transient influences can be variable.

Recognition of wave-type influences upon us, of the element of art form available to our reality, of the limiting impositions within language-genetic accident-social environment—this recognition brings with it a new freedom and independence.

Once I have recognized bad drama, lethal interrelationships, lines that don't play—once I am aware of these things as specific influences—I no longer am responsible for *any* of the scenarios produced by my ancestors or even for the scenarios I wrote yesterday. However, I remain responsible for putting new scenarios on the boards *which don't repeat old mistakes.*

The objective description of our universe rooted in the dogma of classic religions and political theories has broken down. We have been misled by stellar performances from fellow humans—from Solomon to Machiavelli to Nixon, from Hammurabi to St. Paul to Martin Luther to Paul VI, from Confucius to Aristotle to Descartes to Hegel to Freud to Skinner—by stellar performers remembered and unremembered and by a host of satellite performers within their influence.

We have been misled, with accent on *led.*

Leaders require followers, teachers require students, knowers require the ignorant and vice versa ad infinitum. Every dichotomy needs actors (dolls?) who play their parts without question.

We play out the dichotomies to their inevitable contradictions, having chosen and accepted our parts, and when the condition of *conjugate variables* becomes inescapable, when the paired things interfere with each other, we scream "paradox" or give up to despair.

Like the good dolls of *Probable,* we play our parts just

as we were designed to do within the orderly confines of *Reality*.

But those fleeing *refugees* and the *forces* from which they fled, the *pilots* and the *targets* in the air war, the maimed *survivors* of napalm and the *makers* of napalm, the *bombardiers* and the *living things* killed by the new concussion bomb, the Belfast *bombers* and the dead *child*, the murdered *policemen* and the *murderers*, the *guerrillas* and the *10 dead* in the village, the tortured *prisoners* and the *torturers*, the starving American *Indians* and the *officials* of the Bureau of Indian Affairs—all are humans, not dolls. They are a form of animal life indigenous to this planet, to the best of our knowledge. They are highly susceptible to geocentric influences, profoundly dichotomized and polarized.

We possess an unlimited fund of euphemisms with which to filter out the observation that it is fellow humans upon whom we perform our resonating atrocities.

Many clues to the filter systems provided us by *Reality* remain in our symbols—in euphemisms, in verb constructions, in gestures and other actions, in unexamined assumptions behind some of our more commonly accepted terms.

Take the word *knowing* for example. Here's a remarkable filter. When I *know* a thing, I am efficiently insulated from any disturbing questions which might throw doubt upon my *position*. *Knowing* creates a "bound state" like a satellite tied to its parent body by mechanical forces. The operation of *knowing* can be seen in the ways we create specializations and other compartmentalizing techniques (such as education confined to pre-selected categories) which turn more and more of our destiny over to fewer and fewer experts.

Take the concept of *guilt*.

One of my black brothers recently accused me of oppressing him "for more than 400 years." The accusation was based on the observable fact that my skin is white.

Now, I haven't been around for 400 years, worse luck,

but I have been around long enough to research this question farther back than 400 years. I have news for my black brother. Whites have been oppressing blacks and blacks oppressing whites for a helluva lot longer than 400 years.

And do my researches turn up a load of guilt for him!

The elite black troops brought into Spain by the Moors used to ride into a Spanish village, tie up all of the inhabitants, slaughter the children in front of their parents, rape all of the women, then wipe out the survivors by slow torture.

The trouble with this *knowledge* applied as a guilt-weapon is that a little additional research into ancestral probabilities reveals the disturbing item that my black brother and I each had ancestors on both sides of those atrocities.

If you can trace any ancestors back to the Mediterranean littoral (placing absolute confidence in the breeding habits of your great grandmothers *and* their progenitors), then it is a high likelihood that you have a mixture of black, white and semitic ancestry no matter the present shape of your nose or color of your skin. While you're tracing, don't forget that the Phoenicians traded far and wide from their Mediterranean bases, that the Hanseatic merchants brought back more than merchandise, and that some survivors of the Spanish Armada lived long enough in Ireland to leave genetic tracks.

Like good dolls, we're still playing the dichotomy games, choosing sides, resonating. One of our weapons-filters is *guilt*; another is *knowing*.

What do I really know?

What are the visible consequences of past "good works"? (How *did* we come by that pejorative label: "do-gooder"? What did someone say the road to hell was paved with?)

Isn't it possible for us to laugh at ourselves even a little bit when our own best efforts go awry? Having laughed at ourselves, isn't it then possible to answer the demands for change? Haven't we learned yet that extended "stability" represents a lethal form of existence?

In a *possible* universe with multi-level systems, influences of and consequences of our actions can be deceptive, and the scientist who says the simpler of available answers always is to be preferred may be misleading himself and us. Operational evidence which is not subject to continual monitoring and projection of consequences can lead us into lethal cul-de-sacs. Trying to control the future in absolute terms "for all time" tends to make *any* future at all less and less likely for humans. Absolutist logic based on determinism fails when confronted by Infinity.

A reading of our present condition indicates that our reality factory is profoundly out of step with our universe. Perhaps the human mind isn't well adapted (or conditioned, or aimed, or channelled, etc.) to view its own involvement in the systems which influence (resonate) it— including the system represented by the language with which I articulate such ideas. Perhaps our concept of knowing, of control and power, needs to be modified by a concept of mutual influences and fluid consequences. The ancient Greeks may have been correct when they spoke of humours. They meant *wet* or *flowing* by the term. It signified movement and change.

Let's try another postulate:

Postulate VI: Simplistic, stabilized, absolute and fixed views of reality (frames of reference) always interfere with our view of the future.

Everything we do can be traced to microscopic events. The deeper we probe into that microscopic universe, the more and more difficulty we encounter in predicting the future of isolated phenomena. One of our problems in developing an Infinity Logic is the inescapable conclusion that, in an infinite framework, *we* are microscopic events. Our problem can be stated this way:

To develop sufficiently extended mass-time-energy frameworks it is necessary that we become macroscopic and thus subject to probability patterns.

When we come in big enough packages, you can predict our behavior.

We appear to occupy a potentially definable spectrum in an infinite system where the potential and the definitions change as we expand the limits of our view.

It is only in the macroscopic world that we have found future behavior of probability systems to be determined by their past. Only when we get a big enough view of the dynamics of a system have we been able to tell how it performs.

Then how is our reality factory out of step? We have stored data for centuries. We have accumulations of observations which span thousands of years. We are making our first toddler's steps toward world government. We have large associations and corporations.

But no one is putting it all together.

The creative genesis of new and larger frames of reference has been sidetracked while we devote greater and greater energy to specializations of narrower and narrower focus. Academic research is dominated by the "bit which I can encompass in my lifetime." Research in other areas is dominated by corporate security of various denominations from Merck & Co., Inc., to the State of France. Each seeks that transient myth, *the competitive edge*. And every competitive edge (based as they are on the inevitable contradictions of dichotomy) dissolves in disaster. The stirrup escalates cavalry until it encounters a see-saw standoff against armor and castles until these dissolve before logical developments along the gunpowder line until all are crushed by the energy within the atom.

Finally, no piece of real estate can be defended with absolute security. (There never was such a defense anyway.)

We have awakened to a new age in which chemical and bacteriological warfare put mass murder into the hands of small groups operating with a few thousand dollars from basement laboratories. There exists a sufficient number of psychotic frames of reference in our world to insure that such operations already are under way. And the high probabilities in technological research promise us even greater horrors for as long as we operate from a reality which assumes the absolute reliability of narrowing dichotomies as a way of life.

It appears that any path which continues to narrow our possibilities represents a lethal trap. The model of a humankind which threads its nervous way through an infinite maze can be the dominant aspect of our universe only for creatures with noses to the ground, following a simplistic track. Physics, mathematics and philosophy over the past two decades have shot this view of an either/or universe so full of contradictions that it now presents us with the appearance of a swiss cheese. No matter how you cut it, the slices contain holes.

In such a universe, specialists continue to stake out their exclusive slices (holes and all) from which to say: "You cannot discuss my specialty unless you come up the same track I did."

Attempts to create interdisciplinary bridges between existing specialties tend to stir up specialists the way a shovel stirs up an ant hill. Of the many U.S. university attempts to set up interdisciplinary systems over the past twelve years, the only doctoral level effort to survive, that at Syracuse in Humanities, remains under continuing attack. All of the others, beset by severely limiting restrictions and constant efforts to eliminate them, have produced little impact upon academia. Renewed interdisciplinary efforts in higher education, dating back some three years and aimed at extensive reforms with greater impact, must pass through an administrative gantlet which is essentially unchanged from twelve years ago.

(While you're contemplating this state of affairs, please note the dichotomies awaiting the unwary in *inter*disciplinary and in *bridge*.)

The behavior of many specialists at interdisciplinary conferences is particularly revealing. They tend to gravitate toward their own kind. They tend to show up only for the readings of those papers which "relate to my field." They tend to behave in microscopic ways against a macroscopic background. And every one of these actions can be defended with sound logic from a consistent frame of reference.

It is this very consistency and any frame of reference (reality) which it supports that I am holding up for questioning and suspicion. It isn't so much the either/or approach which traps us as it is the way we hold on to our *discoveries*.

On a human-crowded world where our own population represents a high energy system, the life expectancy of any consistent position can be expected to grow shorter and shorter. Quantum leaps in energy predict this. Remember that it is large numbers of events which give us probable results. It is with large enough numbers that we have developed a degree of accuracy in predicting the future. We may not be dolls, but we occupy the land of *Probable*. Our insurance statisticians tell us: "I can't say whether you're going to have an accident next year, but I can predict how many people of your age and income will have accidents."

The time has come for us to suspect simplistic dichotomies to which we have clung for long periods. (Crime prevention *has* created increases in crime; medicine *has* increased sickness, and religions of peace *have* fostered violence.) This is a time for courageous movement and a profound change in our attitude toward the *overview*, that it too represents process and movement.

We have more than enough data to describe existing conditions. We understand our problems all too well. It is time now to recognize that a full description of all those disconnected, short-term responses we are making to our problems is also a description of how we maintain our problems. Indeed, to make our problems worse, we need only continue present response patterns.

Our consensus reality is demonstrably unreal; it isn't working. We have not developed an operationally reliable logic for Infinity. We are afraid of Infinity in its rawest form because even to think about it takes us through a period when each of us is no longer here. In a sense, most humans peer outward through the overwhelming dichotomy of their own mortal existence and scream:

"If I have to go, I don't care who I take with me!"

A "budding intelligence" (after Piaget) constructs its external world of causal relationships and permanent objects through such a filtering system and out of a demand for the comforting reassurance that "I can stave off disaster."

Out of this narrowing view, I believe we have developed a world society which fulfills the essential requirements for a psychotic organism, including transference relationships (unconscious mutual support of destructive behavior) with those who say they are solving our problems.

Explosive disorientation describes a dominant condition already at work in our world, not from the actions of "guilty people," but from systems which we accept as our limits. We stumble from psychotic break to psychotic break within these unworkable systems, and each break is larger, more violent and more degrading than the one before it.

Thomas More, who put the word *Utopia* into our language by attaching that label to his literary *perfect island*, died of a disease called *man*. (He refused to agree with a psychotic tyrant and was executed.) We still are trying to play More's game by his rules and under conditions where the disease which killed him is even more virulent.

If I am to talk about *utopian futurism* (my avowed purpose here) then I must begin by explaining why I believe we have set up lethal systems of resonance which, if they continue undamped, make it highly probable that we soon will destroy this planet and every living thing on it. In the land of *Probable*, the resolution of this dichotomy is our primary problem because a failure to solve for extinction negates all other problems. Given the survival of our species as the issue at stake, if we then play idle word games around improbable consequences which ignore this stake, that clearly describes a symptom of the insane fragmentation which we have identified as schizophrenia.

My first requirement for a sane futurism begins with the simple statement: *I am not here to participate in the destruction of a world where I have (or hope to have) descendants.* When I raise my gaze to Infinity, I see that a species which incorporates consciousness need not be mortal, need not die.

From this beginning, simplicity evaporates. All of us may not be fertile, but *descendant* already has broad meaning and infinite implications.

If we are surfboard riders on an infinite sea, then when the waves change we adjust our balance. The most dangerous condition is that of imbalance. In the midst of infinite waves, we must gauge as many of them as we can detect and influence them for species survival wherever we can. For a species balancing in such a universe, unanswerable questions which perpetuate self-limiting systems represent lethal danger. We know how we blind ourselves—by fixed roles, by dropping filters over our senses and forgetting them, by locking ourselves into tighter and tighter orbits, by turning our gaze away from creative interaction with an infinite playground which offers itself for our most artistic expressions. The demand of this dichotomy is loud and clear. That human Phoenix Ezra Pound said it: "Make it new."

Those Wonderful Years

BARRY N. MALZBERG

I

Listening to the great sounds of '63, pouring like fruit from the transistors, the engine on high, pulling me irresistibly toward that simpler and more reasonable time of my life. *All is love/stars above/know the tune/I lost so soon*, Cosmo and the Pearls, got it together in '61, got the sounds right the following year, hit it to the top with MOONSONG in that golden year of the assassination and then it all fell apart as so many lives have fallen apart during the 60's: drugs, divorce, abandonment, flight, hatred and Cosmo himself died in a fountain in Las Vegas or was it a pool in '69, must have been around that time, maybe a year later. Does not matter. Old Cosmo was finished by the mid-sixties, the whole sound that he exemplified, the tender lyric which he probed overtaken by harsher jolts but ramming the Buick at high speed down the expressway it is '63 again and Cosmo is young, all of us are younger and I let the apples and oranges of that music bounce over me, humming only a little at the rhythm parts. On the expressway I whir past other aspects of the past: cars from the early sixties assault me from oncoming lanes, yield to me on the right and in the chrome, the strange, bent archaic shapes of the 60's I know my history again and again revealed. MOONSONG ends on a diminished seventh or maybe it is merely a hanging chord (I know absolutely nothing about music other than how it affects me) and the radio is still, then there is a commercial for the Wonder Wheel chain of superior foodstuffs in the metropolitan area and without transition from '66 comes the sound of the TROOPERS singing *Darkness of Love*. '66 was a good year too although not as critical in many aspects as '63, still it is a period worth remembering. The TROOPERS help me remember. Locked to the sound, a little pivot wheel of memory I soar through all the spaces of the Expressway and into the impenetrable but to-be-known future. The vaginal canal of the future, parting its thick lips for me gently as I snaffle along in pursuit of my destiny.

II

Outside the building containing Elvira's single-girl's apartment I wedge the car into a space, remove the key (cutting off Tom and the Four Gees in SWEET DE-LIGHT, a pure pear plucked from the tree of '54, a little before my time but no matter) and sit behind the wheel for a moment, meditating. I am a little early for our date which happens quite often but then too I am in no hurry to see Elvira, preferring always to cherish the memories gathered through our times together than to go into the difficult business of creating new ones. (The past is fixed, the present incomprehensible, the future without control; I must remember this.) Already Elvira is an artifact to me; her breasts already seem to have the glaze of embalming fluid, her mouth tastes like mucilage, it is not Elvira which I am kissing so much as the Elvira which I will remember. It is difficult to explain this. It is difficult to explain this but I will try: Elvira and our relationship are to be a golden oldie of the early eighties. Thinking this and other muddled thoughts I step briskly from the car, move through stones and into the lobby of the building where I see she has already come down to wait for me, a handbag slung over her shoulder, a tight and aggressive expression across her eyes and cheeks. I know that I will have to suppress memories of Elvira's aggression in order to be truly moved by her years hence. "We must make a decision," she says, grasping my arm between wrist and elbow, in the vicinity of the ulna, and applying modest pressure. "We cannot go on this way. Tonight we must resolve our relationship."

"I am not prepared to make any decisions, Elvira," I say, submitting to her grasp. In ordinary life I am a claims examiner for a large insurance company which has, partly because of me, one of the lowest payout rates in the business, a statistic which they do not advertise. In that capacity I must do a great deal of writing and checking but fortunately this is with the *right* hand and not with the left which feels Elvira's pressure. Resultantly I do not protest at being greeted by her in this way but try to take a lower key. Cosmo and the Pearls, according to the newspaper stories at the time of their success, are supposed to have met on an unemployment line in the Bronx, New York, but I do not believe this. I discard most public biographies as lies and, trusting nothing, believe that the truth can only be found in what Cosmo does to me. A little snatch of MOONSONG buzzes through my head like an indolent fly and I do not slap at it; I listen. *Lost so soon/all I loved/like the stars above.* Above, above. "We will have to take it as it comes, Elvira," I add liking the sound of her name. *El-vi-ra*; it carries within it the characteristic sound of the seventies, posturing and yet somehow childlike, which will surely characterize this decade in the years which lie ahead.

"No," she says, tightening her grasp on the arm, leading me toward the one voluminous couch which in shades of orange and yellow dominates the lobby of her residence, "it cannot be. You've equivocated too much. I can't waste these important years of my life on someone who doesn't even know his identity!" She raises a fist to her face, dabs at her eyes. "And besides that, I sometimes think that you don't even really want me," she says, "that when you're with me you're already thinking about how you'll remember me. I tell you, this is no way for a relationship to function. I have a great deal to offer you but it must be within the terms of the present. You've got to be here with me now."

"You don't understand, Elvira," I say, guiding her to the couch, gently easing down and at last her terrible grip eases and I run a fervid hand over my joint, relocating the source of circulation and bringing the blood to clear surge yet again. "The past is fixed, the present incomprehensible, the future without control. If we repudiate our past, well then, what are we? And if we do not cherish the past, that only immutable part of us, well, then, Elvira, what will we make of the present and the future?" but even as I am saying this I feel the hopelessness of the argument overwhelm me. Her little face is set tight, her little breasts jut with argumentation; if I touched her body my hands would recoil, I am sure, with a metallic spang. She does not understand. Slowly I disengage myself from her, stand, walk back through the lobby, gesticulating.

"I'm not ready to make a commitment," I say, "how can we know where we're going until we know where we've been? you've got to understand history, otherwise the sheer accumulation of data overwhelms," and so on and so forth, now I am beyond the doors themselves, the cool, dense ~laze of air hitting me, ruffling my cheeks and still Elvira sits on the couch, unmoving, her hands closeting her pocketbook, her eyes fixed straight ahead. She seems to be speaking but I cannot hear a word which she is saying. She mouthes polysyllables, I concentrate, but all is beyond me. "I'm sorry," I say, "truly sorry," and walking back to the car feel a fine, true instant of regret; I could come back to her, vault against her on the couch and confess my sin: that dark, unspeakable stain which radiates from the heart through all the tendrils of the body, that stain which begins in loss and ends in acceptance but what good would it do me? Or her? No, our relationship is obviously finished, I restore myself to the seat cushions of my car, hurriedly start the motor and drive away, the radio, caught in the gears, booming.

The Four Knights, '59, THE TEARS OF YOUR HEART. '59 was a year of great transition just as this has been; everything hurt in '59, I let the music run over me like blood and for an instant it is that year again and I twenty years old trying to come to terms with matters which I do not even remember. In retrospect I glimpse Elvira; she remains on the couch, she is sunk on the couch like stone: already a perfect artifact nestled in mucilage, on display for the *tourista* of recollection which in little fibers I shall send on their way in all of the years to come.

III

A man with all of his limbs torn off by an automobile accident was denied compensation when I was able to establish through delicate interviewing and piecing together of evidence that the accident was self-caused and therefore not covered under the terms of his particular policy. For this I was given praise by my supervisor and a small bonus but I cannot get over an unreasonable feeling of guilt even now as if somehow it would have been better if I had falsified the interviews and documentation and allowed the quadruple amputee to slip a false claim through the company.

IV

A Festival of Revival is held at the large municipal auditorium which I attend. All of the great performers of the '50's excepting only those who have died or have gone on to better things are there: the Chryslers and the Flyers, Lightnin' Joe and the Band, the Little Black Saddle, Tony Annunzio. Seated in the third row orchestra, surrounded by stolid citizenry who have carried forward the menacing expressions of their youth and little else, I am stunned again by the energy of that decade, its fervor and wildness, the way in which it anticipated and sowed the seeds of so much else to come, but I am also humbled because in a critical way I have come such a short distance from that time; my responses to the Little Black Saddle are as they were when I was thirteen, no difference, this is no Festival of Changes. Of course the '60's were even more significant than the '50's, I must remember that, and that is to take nothing away from the '40's which prefigured both of these decades to say nothing of the '70's, fast receding from us and likely to be remembered as the most moving decade of all. Tony Annunzio takes off his jacket and tie to sing his final numbers, just as he did in the old days, and I am shocked at how round he has become although, of course, my memories of him are unreliable. His great hit, BROKEN CHAIN OF CIRCUMSTANCE, is the finale of the show and while standing in tribute with the rest of the audience I find myself thinking of Elvira. If only we had been able to share this moment together! but she declined my invitation, of course, hanging up the phone on me nastily but not before saying that in her opinion my unusual attachment to certain elements of the past only showed a childish inability to face the future.

How could I have explained to her that the past *is* the future? and what difference would it have made, the spotlight on Tony Annunzio winking off, the houselights surging on and all five thousand of us rising as one to cheer the voice of his generation, and Tony, standing on the bare stage to take those cheers with the same grace and offhandedness with which, more than twenty years ago, he bowed to us at the old Orpheus, now the *new* Orpheus and also the site of many great revivals?

V

Coming home I find Elvira lying naked in my bed, the covers below her waist, her eyes bright with malice. Try as she may, it seems that she simply cannot leave me alone. I know the feeling well although I have never had it with Elvira. "I'll tell you about the nostalgia craze and your golden oldies," she says with a mad wink, "I've been thinking this through carefully and now I'll tell you the truth." She is thirty-one years old, attractive but not exceptional and from the beginning of our relationship she might have regarded me as her last chance. This has led to much bitterness in the breakup.

"Let me tell you what I think it is," she says, her voice wavering, her little breasts shaking, the nipples pursed as if for a kiss, "the nostalgia craze, this constant digging up of the past for people like you who can't face the future; it's all a government plot. It comes from the capital. They're manipulating everything by digging up the past so that people aren't able to bridge the distance between the present and the future. They think that they can keep people from seeing what's really been *done* to them if they feed them the past like a drug to keep on reminding them of what they used to be. They're going to keep us all locked in the past so that we won't really ever see what's going on *now* but I won't fall for it and I won't let *you* fall for it." She leaps from the bed, breasts shaking, and seizes me around the neck, gathers me in. "Please," she says, "you must face your life, must face what you've become and where you're going, you can't live in the past," moving her body like a lever against mine, bone to bone, flesh to flesh and for all of my embarrassment and rage it is difficult to suppress desire—Elvira and I always did have a good sexual relationship, I have saved certain memories of it and bring them out now one by one in privacy to masturbate—but suppress desire I do, hurling her from me.

"Don't you ever say that," I say to her, "the past is immutable, the past is strong and beautiful, the past is the only thing we have ever known," and resist as she may, I convey her shrieking from bed to wall to door, pausing to guide her fallen clothes with little kicks toward the exit. At the door, I pull the knob with enormous speed and strength and then throw her, weeping, into the hall, kicking her clothes after her. "Get out of here, get out of my life, get out of my way," I say to her and not bothering to gauge the effect which these words have had, slam the door closed and lock it, turn my back to it trembling and then stride toward the radio.

Turning it on to the station of the golden forever I hope that I will find some music of the '60's which will galvanize me with energy and help me find emotional equivalent in events of the past but something is wrong with the radio; the dial is somehow set toward the only station in the area which plays current hits and in palpitation and dread I find myself listening to the Number Two maker on the charts, something about *Meanies and Beanies*, the tune confusingly disordered to me.

It is too much. I simply cannot cope with it; not this on top of Elvira. I sit on the bed wracked with sobs for a while, whimpering like a dog against the strange music and then in the hall I hear the softest and strangest of noises, as if Elvira had somehow found a key and was insinuating herself within . . . and then as the music tumbles cheerfully on I have a vision and the vision is that not only she but the quadruple amputee who I have serviced have somehow managed to get into my room.

They sing along with the radio, I watch them, the vision turns and I shriek like wind out the other side of that tube. From a far distance then I hear *Meanies and*

Beanies for what it always was; an artifact of that forgotten decade, as the nineties overtake me in sound and the amputee and Elvira roll against one another on the floor, their defeat accomplished as the smooth, dense wax of the embalmer pours from the tubes of the radio to cover them like lava on volcanic ash.

Univac: 2200

CLIFFORD D. SIMAK

He came home along a country lane, with grass growing between the dust-powdered cart tracks, with low stone walls to either side, erected long ago and now crumbling with the years, but with their crumbling hidden by the growth of creeping vines and screened by the bushes that grew along their bases. A verdant countryside stretched on every hand, with sleek cattle in the pastures and the smoke of cottage chimneys trailing up the sky. Larks sang in the grasses and a rabbit popped out of its hiding place along one of the stone fences and went bobbing up the road.

The corridor cyber, Andrew Harrison told himself, had knocked itself out on this one. He hoped it would be allowed to stay for a while, for it was most restful. But he knew it wouldn't stay. They never did. It was as if the cyber had so many patterns that it was in a hurry to get them all used up. Tomorrow, or maybe just a few hours from now, it would be the main street of a sleepy old historic village or a woodland trail or an old Paris boulevard, or perhaps some far-space fantasy. Although he doubted the patterns would ever all be used. He'd lived here—how long?—more than fifty years, and before that more than thirty years on one of the lower levels, and in all that time there had not been a repetition, close approximation perhaps, but never a repetition in the corridors.

He did not hurry. He strolled along sedately. He must be getting close to home and when he got there and had to leave it, he'd miss this country lane. He considered stopping for a while to sit upon one of the crumbling walls and listen to the meadow larks and watch the cloud patterns in the deep blue sky, but today he had no time to sit—today was a busy day.

Up ahead of him he saw the signpost that would have his name upon it and that was as far as he would go, for it marked the door of home. Someone else traveling this lane homeward would see another signpost, but no one else would see it, as no one else would see the one meant for his eyes alone.

He slackened his pace, loitering, reluctant to leave the road he traveled. But slow as he might go, he finally reached the signpost and turned off into the little footpath.

A door opened before him and beyond the door was home.

"Good afternoon, sir," said the cyber, Harley. "I hope you had a pleasant walk. Did you get the tobacco?"

"Very pleasant, Harley, thank you."

"And now . . ." said Harley.

"No," said Harrison. "Absolutely not. No drink, no conversation. Forget your role of the gracious servant. I have work to do."

"But, sir . . ."

"And no ski slope, no fishing stream, no beach, no nothing. Just leave me alone."

"If you wish it, sir," said Harley, considerably offended, "I'll leave you quite alone."

"Some other time," said Harrison, "I'll be quite grateful for your services."

"I am always at your service, sir."

"Where are the others?"

"You have forgotten, sir. They went out to the country."

"Yes," he said. "I had forgotten."

He walked from the entry into the living room and, for the first time in many months, realized, with something of a shock, how small the living quarters were.

"There is no need of size," said Harley. "No need of space."

"That's right," said Harrison, "and even if we needed it, or wanted it, we haven't got the space. And I wish, if it is all the same to you, you'd cut out monitoring me."

"I must monitor you," said Harley, primly. "That is my job and as a functioning, conscientious cybernetic system, I must do my job. For if I did not monitor you, then how might I best serve you?"

"All right, monitor," said Harrison, "but keep it to yourself. Can't you, for the next few hours, manage to be somewhat unobtrusive."

"I would suspect," said Harley, "that there must be something wrong with you, but my medical components come up with nothing more than normal and from that I must conclude that you have no illness. But I must confess to being puzzled. You have never been quite this way before. You reject me and my service and I am disturbed."

"I am sorry, Harley. I have something to decide."

He walked to the window and looked out. The country stretched away, far below—a bit more, he remembered now, than a mile below. A great belt of parkland lay around the tower and beyond the parkland wilderness— recreational space for all who wished to use it. For the land was no longer used, or very little used. A few mines, a few tracts of carefully harvested timber and that was all. After all of this was over, he decided, he and Mary would go west to the mountains, for a holiday.

"Why go?" asked Harley. "I can send you there, or to a place that is equivalent to mountains. It would be the same. You would not know the difference."

"I thought I told you to shut up."

"I am sorry, sir. It is just that my only thought is of your welfare."

"That," said Harrison, "is most commendable of you."

"I am glad you think so, sir."

Harrison turned from the window and went into his workroom. The room was small and crammed with equipment and a desk. The windowless walls closed in on him, but he felt comfortable. Here was his work and life.

Here, for years, he had worked. And was his work now coming to an end? Was that the reason, he asked himself, that he had delayed so long, to hold onto work and purpose until the very end? But he was not, he knew, being honest with himself; it was because he must be certain and on that trip down to the retail levels to buy himself a tin of tobacco, it had come to him that he was as certain now as he would ever be.

He grinned, remembering that trip—a hookey trip. There had been no need to go. He could have simply dialed his purchase and a moment later picked it out of the delivery chute. A man, at times, he told himself, will practice self-deceit. If he had wanted to take a walk, there would have been nothing in the world to prevent his taking it. If he had wanted to get away from these small, cramped rooms and Harley, there would have been nothing that could stop him. There had been no need to concoct an excuse to do so.

"I must remind you, sir," said Harley, "that there is never any reason for you to remain in what you think of as these small, cramped rooms. If you would but allow me, sir, I could place you on a lonely mountaintop, all alone upon it, with all the world to see and no one else about, with as much space and freedom as any man might wish. It is because of such as I that humans require little living space. Granted, without the cybers these kind of quarters would be intolerable, but you need not live within them, no *need* to live within them, for the entire world and more is yours. Anything that a cyber can dream is yours and I really do believe . . ."

"Cut it out," said Harrison, sharply. "Another word from you and I'll phone replacement. Perhaps you have been too long in operation and . . ."

"I'll be silent, sir," said Harley. "You have my promise on it."

"See you do," said Harrison.

He sat easy in the chair behind his desk and the questions hammered at him: Could he be entirely certain? Had he overlooked some factor that should be considered? Had he carried his simulations into the future as deeply as he should? There was no doubt at all that the process would work. He had checked the process and the theory step by step, not once, but many times, and there was no question that the procedure and the theory were correct. Now it was no longer a matter of procedure, but a matter of effect. Could he be certain that he could chart the future course of mankind, with this new factor introduced, with enough precision to be sure that it would not produce social aberrations that might not be evident for centuries?

Future history, he reminded himself, could be changed by such unlikely items that one could take no chance at all.

Take the present world, he thought, take the mile-high cities and all the vacant acres, and one could trace it back to so short a time as two centuries before. A man could put his finger on the time when it began, marking the break with a cultural pattern that man had laboriously put together in five millennia of effort. Two hundred years ago man had lived in noisome cities that had stretched across mile on mile of land; today he lived in towers that scraped the very sky. Now, instead of industrial centers and power plants belching smoke and gobbling up the dwindling resources of the earth, man got his energy from fusion and needed only a fraction of the power he had needed then because he did with very little.

There had been no need, he told himself, for the change to have been as great as it had been; there had been those, history reminded one, who had thought of it all as madness. The idea had been carried farther than there was any need by the great revulsion that had risen at the olden way of life and this revulsion, a madness in itself, had swept all mankind beyond the point of common sense. And yet, perhaps, he thought, it was just as well, for because of it man had, in many ways, a better life and a cleaner planet.

He tried to imagine how it might have been in those days when the rivers ran dirty to the sea and the sea itself was foul, when the air and earth were poisoned and a great noise beat against the land.

The world in which he sat, he thought, had begun to form with the first pollution-killed fish that floated to the surface, with the temperature inversion that had blanketed a city with the smog that it had spawned, with the cry of rage that had gone up against the smoking chimneys and the streams of effluents that were poured into the waters. We must built new cities, men had screamed, and the new cities had been built, but not quite the kind the screamers had envisioned; we must halt the overuse of resources, other men had shouted, and in time the old, time-honored rule of obsolescence had been scrapped and commodities had been built to last— not for ten years or twenty, but for centuries. As a result of this, in time fewer commodities were manufactured and the use of natural resources and energy had diminished and there had been less and less pollution and today the rivers ran crystal to the sea and the air was clean and fresh and the land lay quite unpoisoned since agriculture had been moved indoors and no longer utilized the soil.

A city, he thought. Once a sprawling mass of structures, today three great towers: one for residential purposes, another for agriculture and industry, the third for services—for government, education, arts and sciences, recreation. Three great towers reaching deep into the earth, rearing far into the air, and all operated by electronic wizardry. A people served by cybernetic systems that turned bleak corridors into country lanes, that gave a man an authentic simulation of every possible environment, that did one's chores and wiped one's nose and helped to do one's thinking and placed at each man's fingertips all the knowledge in the world.

And all of this, he thought, because a crackpot (the first of many crackpots) a bit more than two hundred years ago had bellowed out a maniac conviction that the earth was being poisoned.

From that first crackpot to this, so small a thing to bring about so great a change.

And that was why, he told himself, he must be absolutely certain.

He rose from his chair and went to the console, lifted the think-piece from its cradle and put it on his head. Sitting down in the operator's chair, he punched in the gross knowledge components, then fed in the factors. He had done it all before, he told himself; he would do it all again. It was not necessary, he was sure; he already knew. But in a thing like this nothing must be left undone.

It was all imagination, of course, but he seemed to see and be aware of, as had happened many times before, the great banked cores of all the knowledge banks that now were open to him—medical at Mayo's in Minnesota, legal at Harvard, theology in Rome, sociology at California and history at Yale, all these and many more.

And it was not only knowledge. Knowledge in itself was not sufficient. It took more than that; it required the thought enhancement that was electronically built into the instrument. Man and computer now, human brain and robot brain, working in tandem, hooked into the basic banks of the world's entire hoard of knowledge, with the waiting relays that would open the way to other banks of knowledge should they be required.

Now that all was ready, he asked the question: What

would be the long-range effect of intellectual immortality upon the human race? What if the minds of men could be transferred and imprinted upon robotic brains?

But that was not entirely right, of course. You would not imprint a human mind upon a robot brain, then range the brain upon a shelf with other brains and leave it there. You'd mount the brain upon some sort of ambulatory device that would serve the function of a body. You'd have, to some degree, a robotic body, perhaps extremely sophisticated, much more sophisticated than a human body, with many skills a human did not have, and yet it would not be, in many aspects, human. So you'd have intellectual immortality and, in a way, physical immortality, but not human immortality. To become immortal, a man must become a robot.

What was wrong with that? he asked himself. Where lay that nagging flaw? Why was he so reluctant to reach a fast decision? What was it that sent him back again, and yet again, to a simulation of the situation?

Man lived in a computer world, a robotic world, a cybernetic world. Every chore that man could think of was performed, upon command, by cybers. Most of his needs and wishes were fulfilled by cybers. The city in which he lived, the very home in which he lived was a cybernetic system. Men lived easily and comfortably with electronic contraptions and were happy with them. He trusted them and valued them and looked to them not only for his comfort, but for his happiness. The cybernetic system that was one's home could simulate another environment for one with precise exactitude. It could send you to a beach and it would not be just an impression of a beach, the suggestion of a beach. It would be a beach. You would feel the sand beneath your body, would feel the sea-wind blowing, would know the heat of sun, would hear the sound of surging water and be wetted by it. You would be upon a beach, not pretending you were there, not imagining you were there. You would be really there. It need not be a beach. It could be a forest, a mountaintop, a desert, a jungle, a raft upon the sea, the moon or Mars. It could send you back through time to dwell in a castle on a Rhine, to labor in the fields with serfs on a medieval manor, to participate in a joust upon a field of honor, to sail with a Viking crew.

If one could live with and accept such fantasies as these (an easy thing to do, for they did not seem like fantasies), then why recoil from a fact that was no fantasy— that man, if he chose, could live forever? The robotic brain, or robotic body could not be a part of human rejection of or revulsion against such a situation, for in those simulations of other times or places to which one most willingly subjected himself, he became as intricately, or perhaps more intricately, involved with robotic functions.

Harrison sat before the console and as the thoughts built up within him, he felt, just beyond his reach, but available if he should need to reach out for them, the phantoms of all the massive portions of knowledge packed in the knowledge centers. As if, massed solidly behind him, were all these men, all these thinkers of the ages who had preceded him, standing ready with all their knowing and their counsel. A continuity, he thought, a great human continuity that spanned from the present day back to that old prehistoric ancestor who had come to terms with fire, to that sub-human creature that had struck two flints together to construct a tool. And that, he told himself, was a part of it as well. The minds of men were a resource and here were being used, but in each individual case, a resource with a lifetime limited to less than a century (although now, in this year of 2218, the old limit no longer held and a man, barring accident, could confidently expect to live a century and a half). But that was something new, just as immortality would be something new. And if human minds were a resource, why allow them to be limited by time? Why be content to use a mind for a century and a half and then be content to see it die? Certainly the human minds imprinted upon robotic brains would continue to contribute to humanity and the continuity of the human mind would be that much strengthened.

He did not sense the others moving in, but he knew they had moved in and he closed his eyes and was in a peopled darkness. There was a voice, speaking in the darkness, and that was strange, for in all the times before there had been no voice.

Second-class citizen? asked the voice and it seemed that he was rolling from the darkness, not walking from it, but rolling from it. And it seemed instead of rolling that he was scuttling, moving furtively, afraid of being seen, shrinking from the ridicule if he should be seen, knowing that in this human world he could not be human who had been human once. Although it seemed strange that he should feel this way, for the very ones who scorned him and reviled him in some later day might become as he.

Dead conservatism? asked the voice in the darkness and when the voice spoke he was no longer rolling, but was huddled in the darkness—a huddled machine among many other huddling machines and as he huddled there he heard the mumblings of his fellows and while he could not make out the words he knew what they said and from this he knew that they were huddling not only in the darkness, but in the past as well. There were the huddling machines, but there were others that were not machines, but rather immobile brains sitting in rows upon the shelves that stretched up and down this place wherein he huddled and these shelved brains seemed more content than those that had the bodies.

Death in life? the voice asked and when the voice stopped another voice spoke, a low and husky voice that belonged to the machine standing close beside him. Humanness, it said to him and all the others there, is not the matter of the mind alone, of the intellect alone. It is, as well, a matter of the body, of the women that we loved or the men we loved, of the things we ate, of lying on a hillside and feeling the earth beneath us and seeing the top branches of a great oak tree against the cloud-flecked sky, the feel of flesh on flesh when we shook hands with a friend, the smell of evergreen at Christmas, the glories of the lilies in the Eastertide . . . The low, husky voice went on and on, but he no longer heard it; he had shut his ears against it. It was saying all he felt and he did not need to hear and he did not wish to hear.

But would it be that way? Need it be that way? Why must these old bogeys rise? Could not humans accept their roboticized members, not as bogeymen, not as aliens, not as harsh reminders of what the future held for each of them, but as a metamorphosis, another way of human life, the only way of human life if there were to be survival? It was either that or death. Surely, on the face of it, anything was preferable to death. Not that death, in itself, was bad, but it was oblivion, an emptiness, an ending and a nothingness and certainly man had a right to expect something more than nothingness.

Unless, he thought—unless there could be something to an afterlife. What if persisting as a human intellect should rob a man of an afterlife? But there was, he thought, no evidence, no evidence at all, that there was such a thing as afterlife. And the thought brought a clamor in his mind—a quarreling clamor from all those others with him.

When the clamor died down, he tried to think again. Perhaps, then, the thing to do was to investigate the theory of an afterlife. But how would one do that? How could one go about it? What kind of investigative process should one use, how could one evaluate the data, how could one be sure the principles applied to that evaluation would be valid?

He reached up and tore off the headset, thumbed the console back to deadness. What the use, he thought. How could one be ever really sure?

He rose, shaken, from the chair, and went back to the living room. He stood before the window, but now there was nothing he could see. Clouds had moved in far below him and masked the landscape.

"A drink, sir?" asked Harley. "I think you need a drink."

"I think I do," said Harrison. "Thank you very much."

The liquor dispenser did not ask. It knew exactly what he wanted. He picked up the drink and turned back to the window.

It made no sense, he knew. It was all old prejudice and bias. Man had the right to expect a shot at immortality, if it were possible. And it was possible. Perhaps not in exactly the form that one might want it, but it was available. It was there and could be had.

The wastefulness, he thought, the utter wastefulness of death. If for no other reason, immortality would recommend itself on economic grounds. But no matter what might be decided, the old objections would still persist; they never went away. If he had stayed longer at the console, the favorable opinions would have wiped away and set at naught all but a tiny nagging doubt that would hang on forever. There was little use, he told himself, in returning to the console. The pattern had been set and it would not change.

He had gone, he knew, as far as he could go.

He went back into his workroom and sat down, not in the console chair, but behind his desk.

"Harley," he said, "please get me Univac."

"Surely, sir," said Harley.

In front of him a shimmer came, that shimmer no amount of work and research ever could get rid of, and the face was there. No body, as would have been the case if it had been a human, but just a face hanging in the air. It could as easily have been a human face, with body, Harrison reminded himself, a human simulation of the mighty system that was, in fact, the city, but the system itself had not gone along with that. "Let us be honest," it had said and it still was honest—not a human, but a system. And in accord with that it was not a human face that stared across the desk at him, but a strangely mechanistic face, the sort of face than an artist, full of artistic cynicism, might have conjured up to represent the system.

"Mr. Harrison," said Univac, "how good to see you once again."

"It is good to see you, too," said Harrison. "You recall, perhaps, that I spoke with you some time ago about a project I was working on."

"Yes, of course," said Univac. "Immortality. How is it getting on?"

"It can be done," said Harrison. "A human mind can be imprinted. I am sure of that."

"What does the computation say?"

"It says we can imprint. With no loss. No aberration. A human mind can be transferred intact."

"And be effective?"

"Entirely effective. There may be, eventually, some emotional loss. We can't be sure."

"Mr. Harrison, if that should happen, how important would it be?"

"Immensely important from the human viewpoint, perhaps. Although it might make the mind the more efficient, we are not, of course, entirely sure it would come about."

"You, of course, have done exhaustive simulation?"

"Yes," said Harrison, "exhaustive. That's what bothers me. It works out. There would be a period of social adjustment, certainly. At first, perhaps not all the people would wish the transfer. There might always be some who would shrink from it, although, as time went, there would be fewer of them. Perhaps the time would come when it would be accepted as a normal course of human life, a normal event in the life of any man. It might take some time for the public to accept the actual presence of robotic humans—not robots, but humans in robotic form—but that, in time, I am sure, would work itself out. Humanity would gain by it. We would be the richer by each human mind that could be saved from death. Our brainpower would increase, with no great additional drain on our natural resources."

"What is your problem, then?" asked Univac.

"A nagging doubt," said Harrison. "One that hangs in there and will not go away. Based on certain objections that have no real logic in them. They can be explained away, but they stay. It is, I suppose, a matter of human intuition, if not human judgment. I hate to go against human intuition."

"So would I," said the face that was Univac.

"What do we do, in such a case? Wait another century, with men dying all the time, to make up our minds?"

"Some controlled experiment, perhaps."

"But we couldn't do that. Without it leaking out. Can you imagine what might happen if such a thing leaked out? There'd be sheeted hell to pay. The public almost immediately would divide into two hostile groups and the pressure from each group would be unimaginable. It would be an intensely emotional thing, you see . . ."

"Yes, I know," said Univac. "I have something else in mind. You have heard, of course, although it is not yet public knowledge, that in another year or so we plan to send out several interstellar probes."

"Of course. I am a good friend of Anderson. We have talked about it."

"It strikes me," said Univac, "that it might be preferable to send out humans rather than mere instruments. There'd be instruments, of course, but also that other factor you mentioned—human judgment."

"A controlled experiment," said Harrison. "Yes, of course it would be that. And if planets should be found, roboticized human minds could go out onto them, no matter what the conditions were. They'd not have the physical limitations . . ."

"Perhaps," said Univac, "we could send several of them on some of the probes, so that we could study the interaction between several imprinted brains. And on at least one probe, a single imprint, to see how one mind alone could react under . . ."

"It's a vicious experiment," said Harrison.

"Most experiments involving humans are vicious. But it would be a matter of free choice. It would be carefully explained to potential volunteers. To a man on the verge of death, it might be preferable."

"Yes, it might be."

"Then we'd know," said Univac. "We'd know if it would work. The trips would run to a number of years. But we wouldn't have to wait that long. If it appeared to be working, we could engineer a leak about what had been done, then sit back and wait for the reaction. I am willing to wager that in a short time we'd be faced with a wide demand that this business of immortality be made available, immediately, to everyone."

"And if the reaction were the opposite?"

"Then we'd deny the rumor. We'd say it never happened."

"Some day the probes would be coming home," Harrison pointed out. "What about our denial then?"

"By that time," said Univac, "it would be—how do you humans say it—a new ball game."

"May I say something, sir?"

"Why, of course, Mr. Harrison. What made you think that you should ask?"

"It is simply this," said Harrison. "You have shown yourself to be as low-down and sneaky as any human ever was. I would not have thought it of you."

Univac chuckled at him, a ghastly chuckle. "One thing you forget," he said. "Humans made me."

"But that's not good enough," Harrison told him, sharply. "Human is not good enough. We had hoped for something better. We made you, certainly—we built you through the years. We based a culture on you, not, perhaps, because we wanted to, but because we were forced to do so. Perhaps you were no more than the least objectionable alternative, but you were all we had. We had hoped we had acted wisely and perhaps we did. But where we had no alternative before, we have none now. We are stuck with you and you, if you have a personality, an identity, a sense of I, as I think you have, likewise are stuck with us."

"I have identity," said Univac.

"Then, for the love of God," said Harrison, "stop being so damn human."

"Mr. Harrison," asked Univac, "what would you have me be? It was you who created me and . . ."

"We created religion, too," said Harrison. "And what did it ever do for us—the kind that we created? Not one man's concept of God, whatever it might be, but the concept of religion as created by our culture. For years we slaughtered one another in religion's name . . ."

"You created me and used me," said Univac, "for your human purposes."

"And you resent this?"

"No, I do not resent it. I am glad of it and, awkward as it may be for me to say it, rather proud of it. But since we're being truthful, let's be truthful all the way."

"O.K., then," said Harrison, "we created you and used you. We had allowed the profit motive to run away with us. We sold people things they didn't need and we built into these things imperfections so that people bought these things not once, but many times. And we changed the styles and we preached the gospel that one could not be out-of-date without, at the same time, being socially unacceptable. We improved our products and we hammered home the fact that the old models or old styles should be junked for the sake of these improvements, most of which were questionable improvements. And in order to turn out all these things for which we had created a psychological demand, we poisoned our air and water and used up our natural resources and there came a time when we had to call a halt, not to pollution so much as to the economic system that caused pollution, to that factor of our society that was eating up our coal and oil and gas."

"But, if you recall, Mr. Harrison, I also was created by the profit motive."

"That is true, of course. Perhaps it was somehow written in the stars that we must continue with the profit motive until we had developed the capacity for your creation."

"You believe events may be written in the stars?"

"I don't know," said Harrison. "But let us say that somehow, by whatever special dispensation, we were granted a second chance. That second chance was you. Today we live in cities that are you, without great demands being made upon our limited natural resources. Today we specialize in services; we take in one another's washing. None of us is rich and none expects to be. We never think of monetary riches. And I think we may be much the happier for it. So now you must stand with us. If you don't, we're finished. I know there must be a million ways you could bring us to disaster."

"You must mistake me, Mr. Harrison. I have a sense of duty, perhaps of gratitude."

"The thing I must point out," said Harrison, "is that the quickest way for you to ruin us is to strive too much toward humanity. We need someone who thinks a little differently, someone who may understand and sympathize with our human needs and aims, but who can stand off a little distance and tell us when we're wrong and why we happen to be wrong. We would not, as I say, give up human judgment or any shred of our humanity, but now we need someone else, another kind of judgment to balance against our human judgment."

"You think this matter of immortality . . ."

"That's exactly what I mean. I came as close as I could. I think no human could come closer. But there is something, some blind wall, intruding from the human past, that makes human judgment in this area quite impossible. Here we need another kind of judgment, not to negate human judgment, not to rule it out, but to correlate with it. A survey panel, let us say."

"I could think on it," said Univac. "I could let you know. But I feel uncomfortable . . ."

"I know you do," said Harrison. "I know exactly how you feel. Don't you think I feel it, too? I giving up something that was an exclusively human function; you taking on something that is a small step beyond your province. But if we are to make it, if we are to carry on the human dream, each of us must do it. For this is not the only case. This may be the first one, but there will be others, many others as the years go on."

"I hope that you are right, sir."

"I hope so, too," said Harrison.

"I will let you know."

"Thanks," said Harrison. "I'll look forward to it."

The face of Univac faded and Harrison rose from his chair and went into the living room.

"It was a hard day, sir," said Harley.

"Yes, Harley, I think you could call it that."

"And now another drink?"

"That would be very fine."

"You are sure that is all."

"Quite sure. No beach, no ski slope, no . . ."

"I am aware of that," said Harley, hastily. "I thought perhaps a little music."

"I want to think," Harrison said, sharply.

"But man has thought so long," said Harley, "of so many things."

"That is right," said Harrison, "and he's never going to quit. The best that he can hope for is a little help to keep his thinking straight."

He sat in the chair in the tiny living room, with the drink in hand.

Sellout, he wondered, or a big stride forward?

Mommy Loves Ya

DAVID H. CHARNEY

KAREN STOOD behind the twisted steel girder and watched the kids gang up on the old lady. It was a warm, crisp smelling, October day and the naked children screeched with laughter as the old one tried to avoid the rocks and sticks. Each time a rock hit her she would do a spastic dance and the children would double over, holding their sides and gasping for breath. She shook a fist at them, cursing from her toothless mouth.

"Rat meat, rat meat! Not even good enough to eat," the little ones chanted, throwing more sticks and stones.

Karen's son, Tommy, stayed on the outskirts of the crowd. He wasn't laughing with the others. His face kept puckering up. He wanted to cry but was holding it in. Karen had taught him that four-year-olds never cried but Tommy was like his mother, too emotional.

One of the bigger children pushed him forward shouting, "Lookit, lookit!"

The old woman had fallen to her bony knees and was scrambling on all fours trying to get over the camp barrier. The children redoubled their efforts, still laughing, but a hysterical note crept in.

Tommy turned and ran from the crowd, tears stinging his eyes. The sound of chanting followed him. "Rat meat, rat meat! Not even good enough to eat." He ran back to where Karen stood. "Mommy, Mommy," he cried.

Karen felt her own eyes fill with tears. "Tommy," she crooned. "It's all right, honey. Mommy loves ya. Don't cry, it's all right, it's all right."

"Mommy, I'm scared. Why do they do that? Why, Mommy?"

"It's all right, honey. When you're older you'll understand. Come on, dear. Let's go to Daddy."

Karen took Tommy's hand and led the way through the debris. The camp area on Sixty-seventh Street was protected by stone barricades on all sides. Each family of the tribe had its own living unit hidden in the square block. Only the steel girders and heavy cement foundations of the original buildings still stood. Karen went by a tortuous route till she came to her place. She knocked at the entry till her husband let her in.

Harold was one of the strongest of the "midtowners." He and his family ate regularly and his cave was well protected. It was in the foundation of an old building. A trapdoor with a solid drop bolt guarded the entrance. The area was large but dark. Electrical connections were on every wall but no current had run in them for over fifty years. The furniture was sparse, a table of wood and seats scavenged from old car wrecks. The chimney never worked so the room always smelled of stale wood smoke.

Karen was happy there. She had Tommy to love, and Harold was good to her. She had been taken in a raid uptown over five years ago and already her memories of childhood had faded. She was taller and darker than most of the midtowners. Her long, black hair fell over a thin, sensitive face. Her broad cheekbones accentuated the pointed chin. At the ripe age of eighteen, with a child of four, she had no real complaints. Harold was a good provider even if he didn't show the affection she had been used to as a child. She made up for the lack by lavishing attention on Tommy. The boy was a miniature of his mother, reproducing her heart-shaped face and mirroring her emotional volatility.

Harold was eating a rat thigh, the fat making matted patches on his beard. "How come you're back so early?" he asked.

"Tommy didn't want to run with the kids anymore."

"He's getting to be more like you everyday. He'd better toughen up. If he don't somebody is gonna grab him for dinner one day."

Karen made a face. "Things aren't that bad yet," she said. "We've always had plenty of rat meat. I don't like to talk about eating people. I think it's disgusting."

"Your folks, uptown, could afford to feel like that. They had plenty to eat, but when you're hungry for protein, people taste pretty good."

Karen shuddered. "Let's talk about something else," she said.

Harold wiped his mouth with the back of his hand. Karen couldn't help admiring the sleek look of him. Harold was almost fat; no ribs showed and his stomach actually protruded.

"Tomorrow we're crossing town for a meat hunt. One of the scouts found a big rat's nest in a parking garage. There should be enough meat to last into winter."

"Harold, I've got a bad feeling about tomorrow. You be careful."

"You and your feelings." Harold laughed. "They wasted your time teaching you when you were a kid. Maybe I can't read or write but I learned how to hunt and fight. That's what you need in this world."

Karen said, "Someday things will be different again, if

we don't forget we're human. We can have a good world just like it used to be."

"I know the old stories about when cars rolled and men flew. They don't mean a thing now." Harold started polishing his axe as if it were not already gleaming.

Karen sat with her arms around Tommy, watching. "Don't put me down because you have no feelings."

"Hell." Harold raised his axe. "This is the only feeling I have to know. A sharp edge and a good arm."

"Love is more important. Your love for me and Tommy. You do love us, don't you?"

"Karen, you keep saying 'love.' Look around and see what love did to our world. A hundred years ago we had animals, birds, and fish. No more! We killed them all off; now it's just us, the rats, and the bugs. Don't say love to me. You, Tommy, and my axe are all I have; you belong to me and don't forget it."

Harold grabbed her arm and squeezed till her face crumpled in tears. "I don't care what you say," she sobbed. "I love you and always will."

The next day the tribe set out across town. Karen, with the other women and children, brought up the rear, while the male hunters led the way. Scouts ranged ahead of the column checking the abandoned cars that filled the streets. Their neighbors would be happy to pick off stragglers for anything they could get.

In crossing the dead streets the group made regular detours around areas where car bodies blocked the streets. The city had never cleaned up after the violence of July, 2052. In one hot summer week over a hundred thousand cars had been overturned or smashed in the streets. Lack of gas and oil had already made the vehicles almost obsolete, and the week of welfare riots had only hastened the death of the city.

The women kept a constant watch for anything usable as they trailed the hunters, but fifty years of scavenging had left little to be found.

When the group finally reached its goal, Martin, the

leader of the hunters, had the women and children positioned where they could watch but stay out of the way.

The hunters quickly surrounded the underground parking lot. Each exit was covered by at least two armed men. At a signal from the leader, the main group slipped into the Sixty-fifth Street entrance. They started moving through the parked cars, banging on the hoods with their weapons. The noise echoed from the cement walls. Different cars made different notes and the effect was that of a giant orchestra tuning up for a concert. Dust clouds rose from the metal bodies, forming and reforming, as the men climbed by them. The stale smell of rat excrement, carried by the dust, clogged their nostrils.

Most of the cars were stripped down to the barest chassis; every usable bit of leather and rubber had been ripped out. The metal parts were covered with scabrous layers of rust, the paint long gone.

The point man shouted. The first rat had been sighted. The beaters moved faster, starting a pincer movement. They were all shouting now, sweat gleaming on their scrawny, near naked bodies. Karen could see their tangled hair and beards bouncing as they leaped over the wrecks, closing in on the game.

The rat pack swung toward the Columbus Avenue side where Harold was stationed. The men sped up, running along the junk-strewn walkways. A grey flood erupted from the sea of wrecks and poured towards the exit. The rats ranged from six-inch babies to three-foot monsters all blindly driving to escape.

Karen saw Harold's partner swamped in the first wave. He sank silently beneath the tide of hairy bodies. For a moment his kicking feet were visible before he disappeared. The women were all screaming encouragement as Harold swung his axe with demonic fury, holding the rats off till the others could wade in and help.

A giant rodent leaped under the axe blade and sank its teeth into Harold's thigh; its naked tail twitched even after he smashed its skull.

Karen saw Harold's face twist with pain. He pried open

the dead jaws and hobbled along the wall away from the slaughter. "Oh, my God," thought Karen. "He's hurt bad."

Martin blew a note on his horn and the hunters pulled back. There were over sixty dead rats lying by the gateway. A mountain of protein! The tribe fell on the bodies, sorting them into groups and tieing their tails so they could be carried easily.

Harold's companion lay at the bottom of the grey mountain, his throat torn by the rodent teeth.

Karen turned away in disgust as she saw his body added to the food supply. The hunters now moved noisily, but quickly, eager to get the meat back to camp.

Karen picked up Tommy and slipped away. She had seen Harold dragging his bleeding leg to a toll booth, his expression agonized. "My poor dear," she thought, realizing what a serious wound could mean.

Karen knew she would stay with her man, no matter what. She hid in one of the wrecks, whispering over and over to Tommy, "Mommy loves ya. Mommy loves ya."

When the last of the tribe was gone she pulled Tommy to where Harold had disappeared.

"Harold, Harold, are you still in there?" she asked, raising her voice.

"Yes . . ." he called weakly to her.

He had made a tourniquet of his waistband and bandages of the loincloth, using spit to clean the wound. His naked body was covered with a mixture of fine dust and sweat. The area around the bite looked purple and swollen where the poison from the rat's jaws had spread.

"Mommy, I don't like it here," said Tommy.

"Shut the kid up and get in here. I need help."

Karen gasped when she saw the wound close-up. "Lie down," she ordered. Tearing off the dirty bandage, she bent over the thigh and sucked at the poison. She forced the blood to flow again and kept drawing it into her mouth and spitting it out. When she felt it was clean enough she replaced the bandage.

"What'll we do now?" she asked.

"I can't cross town this way. We'll have to wait and see if we can get back tomorrow. Find a place for yourself and the kid. I'll sleep in here."

They were all hungry from the day without food but so tired from the strain of the hunt that sleeping should have been no problem. Karen and Tommy found a booth nearby and the baby fell asleep in her arms. She stayed awake a long time, listening to Harold tossing and turning in discomfort. Eventually he, too, fell asleep and she let herself relax.

The next day Harold walked with difficulty. His leg was swollen and discolored and he complained that his knee was stiff and painful. Tommy, hungry and afraid, was crying constantly. Karen, ignoring her own hunger, helped Harold along the broken streets. The skeleton city hovering over their heads held few dangers except from other men; they made their home block long before dark.

The outpost guard, sighting them from the barricade, called back into the camp. Almost immediately a group of men and boys ran, noisily, to the walls. Martin, the block leader, climbed the barrier and signaled for silence.

"What happened?" he called down.

Harold, hobbling slowly toward the camp, pointed to his leg. "Rat bite," he said. "Pretty bad, but I think it'll be all right soon."

"Stop right there." Martin held up one bony hand. "We can't afford to feed cripples. Protein is too hard to find. Stay away from camp. If you're O.K. next spring, you can come back."

Harold started to protest, but Karen pulled on his arm. "Let's get away from here," she whispered. "I don't trust them."

One of the children behind the barrier threw a rock and, as if on signal, the others started hurling sticks and stones.

Harold, cursing under his breath, wheeled around and hobbled away as fast as he could. Karen pulled Tommy and scrambled after him.

Out of range, Harold stopped and looked back. He shook his fist at Martin's figure silhouetted against the sky. "You bastards. You dirty bastards," he yelled.

Tommy wailed. "Mommy, Mommy."

Harold turned on the child and slapped him across the mouth. "Shut up," he snarled. Karen picked the baby up and tried to comfort him. Harold glared at her and limped off down the street.

They found an old apartment building on West Seventy-fifth Street, with a second floor almost intact, and moved in. There was a gaping hole in the ceiling but the walls hid them from the street and the narrow staircase was easy to protect. Best of all, they found a cache of rags; there were enough to furnish some protection against the winter ahead.

Through October and November Harold managed to kill an occasional small rodent and Karen supplemented the food supply with cleaned and peeled insects. The white inner bodies were edible though tasteless. Tommy cried a lot and Harold grew more irritable as his leg stayed swollen.

As the weather grew colder and the food harder to find, Karen began to fear for their safety. Occasionally groups of hunters passed their home. With the advent of winter human flesh became the staple protein supply of many local tribes.

"Shut him up before I smash his head." Harold's patience wore thinner every day.

"He can't help it. He's only a baby, and he's hungry."

"I don't give a damn. I'm hungry, too. Why do I have to feed that useless little bastard anyway? Shut him up!"

Karen held little Tommy's head in her bands. "Please don't cry," she said. "We'll have lots of food soon. When Daddy is well. Please."

"I'm hungry, I wanna eat," wailed Tommy.

In December, the food supply fell off to near zero. The rodents had dug in and there was no finding them. Insects made up the family's food. Harold sat, day after day, brooding over his stiff leg. He would lean on his axe, glaring at Karen and the baby. All three were now walking skeletons. Harold's stomach had melted away and his ribs washboarded his sides. Their skins broke out and cracked from cold and lack of food.

The December moon shone in through the ceiling. A thin veil of snow drifted through the hole to settle in one corner. Something rattled in the still night air. Karen's eyes snapped open. Harold was sitting up, "Hand me the axe. Quickly!" he whispered. "Keep the kid quiet."

Karen crept over to the sleeping child and put her hand over his mouth. Harold moved painfully to the head of the stairs. He could see nothing but he thought he heard a movement in the dark. He stood, frozen still, trying to force his hearing to reach out like antenna. There was no more sound. After a few minutes he signaled Karen to his side. "I heard someone down there. I'm sure of it," he whispered. "I'm going to try to get down quietly. Keep Tommy from crying. If I don't get back you're on your own."

"Please don't leave us. Wait till morning."

"No chance. I'm going down now. It might be meat."

Harold inched his way down the stairs, stopping to listen on each tread. "Damn," he thought. "If it was a rat, it was a big one and he's gone."

At the bottom, he moved carefully past the booby trap warnings he had set up for intruders. The winter moon cast black shadows on the street level. The light snow and the moonlight made the street luminescent. Harold stopped still. His bare foot had stepped in a patch of wet snow. Something had been there! He slid forward, feet feeling for the wet tracks. "Here it is." He had stumbled on something. He shifted the axe, ready to strike at any movement. Nothing! He reached out to feel the obstacle. It was a human body. No heartbeat, no pulse, no breathing, it was dead but still warm. He dropped his axe and, grabbing the body under the arms, he dragged it to the stairs.

"Karen," he called. "Come here quick."

"What is it?"

"We've got some meat for the winter."

Karen came down the stairs quickly. "Oh, no," she said. "I can't do it. I can't eat human flesh."

"You'll eat it all right. You'll eat it or you'll starve. C'mon, help me get it upstairs."

Between the two, they shuffled the carcass up the stairs. By the shaft of moonlight in the corner they saw the emaciated body of an old man. "Probably thrown out of a local tribe 'cause he couldn't carry his load. Our good luck," said Harold.

In the morning he split the carcass and butchered it into usable sections. His spirits were up for the first time in two months. He cooked and he and Tommy eagerly devoured the tough, stringy steaks while Karen held back and cried.

"I can't do it. I can't," she said as she ate an insect stew.

Harold spent the morning curing the excess meat and laying out parts in the snow to keep fresh. He sang as he worked; even Tommy seemed happier now that his stomach was full.

For the next meal, Harold roasted a leg on a spit. The smell of cooking meat and the sizzle of fat was too much for Karen. She timidly reached out and tried a small piece. Her husband and the baby were wallowing in grease and meat juice, laughing as they ate. The meat was tough but it tasted better than the finest rat meat in the world. Karen ate faster and faster, fat dribbling down her chin. Soon all three were laughing wildly and smearing each other with grease.

The food lasted till February. Harold, Karen, and Tommy spent most of their time huddled together for warmth; their clothing barely kept them from freezing. They had filled out a little, but now, the hunger was even harder to take. The cold outside melted the flesh from their bones; their lips cracked, their eyes became dull, and their skins broke out in sores. Harold went out to hunt less often; his leg had swollen again, making it hard for him to use the stairs. Karen scoured the wrecked buildings for bugs; even they were hard to find. Harold took to sitting hunched over his axe, glaring at Karen and the child. It became more and more difficult to do even the minimum daily tasks.

"We're all going to die." Harold's eyes were fixed sightlessly on the wall and his voice trailed off to a whisper.

"Don't talk like that. We'll make it, I know we will." Karen tried to comfort him.

"We can't all make it. We were lucky before. It won't happen again. This is the worst winter in years; the camps will be using their old people themselves. I don't want to die." His head snapped up and his voice rose to a shout. "I don't want to die. I don't have to die. I can make it."

"Harold, stop it. We'll be O.K. I'll go out and find us something to eat. Don't you worry." Karen smiled through cracked lips. "I feel lucky today. Just you sit quiet till I come back. I have a feeling we'll have something to eat."

Karen bundled Tommy into a corner, making him as warm as she could. "Take care of Daddy," she said.

She went downstairs slowly; weak as she was, movement was painful. "God," she thought. "What can I do?"

The streets were covered with snow. It lay clean and white, scalloped into ornamental ridges by the biting winds. There was no sign of life. She moved listlessly, from building to building, searching the broken foundations. There was nothing to be found. She turned over rock after rock to find only frozen earth.

Eventually she gave up and stiffly worked her way back home.

At the top of the stairs she paused for a moment. A wave of depression swept over her as she took in the scene in the room. Harold was asleep in one corner, his shrunken body propped up against the wall. The extra rags she had used to keep Tommy warm were wrapped around Harold's swollen leg.

Across from him Tommy sat with his knees drawn up

to his stomach, his arms wrapped around his naked legs for warmth. His nude body was blue with cold, his face wet with tears.

Karen moved quietly to Tommy's side. She wiped his face carefully and whispered, "Quiet, honey. Don't make a sound." She went to the axe leaning against the wall.

After she finished with Harold she went back to the baby and wrapped him warmly in the now bloodstained rags. She wiped his tear streaked face. "Don't cry, dear. You'll have your dinner soon. Mommy loves ya," she said.

Peritonitis

GENE WOLFE

Now this is the story Greylock told before the Men of the Neck were scattered forever, before the great exodus and the wandering in the cold lands of hunger. Once (*so said Greylock, my father's mother heard him*) the Men of the Neck ruled all the World and were all the world, and there was nothing between Heel and Finger-tip that was not theirs. In those times a virgin might dine at the Calf and drink at the Eyes and sleep where she would and none would harm her. Then every man said "Brother" or "Sister" when he met a child, and the old were respected. How many were born in those times, and lived each moment of life in those times, and dying rolled away, and never dreamed that the World would not be thus forever? Who can say? Their spirits have gone to the Hair. The dark followed the light for them, and the wettings came and some perished; but this, as all knew, was good lest the People wax too great.

I myself was born into lesser times, but even so not until even those lesser days were nearly ended. I tell you this that you may remember, and know in your despair that God has in times past been good. All is his, all belongs to him alone. Never in the coming time shall you say among yourselves that he has robbed you—what he takes is his; it cannot be otherwise.

No man can now comprehend the joy of those times. There was no bad food anywhere; every morsel was filled with strength, and a happiness indescribable. When the old—yes, even as I am now—ate of that meat their backs straightened and their eyes grew bright; then the grandsire of a thousand might take the goodwife beneath the shade of some soft roof.

And the children of those first times ate, and eating danced in the light, and sang songs that came to them as they sang, one word following another, and played a score of merry games now forgotten, games that grandmothers only mumbled of, forgetting both the names and the rules, even when I myself was but a child; games of running, jumping, hiding and finding, games of hopping, climbing, and singing; games of holding hands in chains.

Again I say, none now can know the joy of those times, and the greatest of them was this—that every man and woman saw, as light came and dark, then light again, and time grew heavy upon them, that that World that was their children's children's waxed.

You do not believe me. Ah, there is no blame in that to you. How could you, who have seen it wane all your lives, yes, and heard your fathers say that it has waned all theirs? But it was true—larger it grew and fairer, the warmth increasing. Then those we call still the New Mountains first began to grow, lifting, very gently then, their slopes above the level plain.

At that time there came a change to the nature of the meat, and none (so have I heard) could well prove whether it was for good or ill—nor can I now say. Happiness it brought indeed, but in that happiness there were a thousand sorrows; yet it was said by many, weeping, that it was a sweeter joy. Then the eaters sang not, but chanted, making of the old, mouth-smoothed words new and unfamiliar things, chants that brought happiness or tears or terror even to those who fasted. And this was called the second age, and it was the time of counterpoint and dreams.

That time too passed. Of the third age what is there to say? You have heard its story already too often. The New Mountains were mighty then, and there came upon all who ate a fever of clean lust that wiped away everything that had gone before. It was then—so I deem it—that the oneness of the People was broken, never in truth to come again. For by twos and threes and fives all but the youngest children drew apart, and those that returned to the gatherings stayed but a little time. At that time if at any the love-promisings that are older than the People were kept: for many a pair dallied all a dark away, and a light too, feasting enough to have fattened a dozen save that love kept them lean.

With the age of New Food that time ended. From the summit of each New Mountain, grown now until they rivaled the Haunches, there broke forth a spring; and the waters of those springs were not clear as the waters of the Eyes are, but white, and sweet. Many a one climbed the New Mountains then to taste of them, though they flowed less than a lifetime. This was the fourth age, and the end of the beginning. For when those springs died the New Mountains waned; and the Belly, which had, scarcely noted, waxed above the Loins, withered in one dark.

Then many felt their doom upon them; this feeling was in the meat, so it was said—but in the air as well. The World was smaller. Then came the Sundering. Some said there was no God; and we, the Men of the Neck, drove them for their blasphemy beyond the New Mountains toward the Loins. Others said that the World itself was God; and these, a fierce and a terrible people, climbed to the Face. Then did we name ourselves Men of the Neck, but beyond our boasting we feared—for though the Men of the Loins might drink there of impure waters, we must needs reach the Eyes when we could eat no more without drinking, and we feared that those above us would prevent us. A few, brave and fleet, ventured first, daring the Spirit Forests to come to the lakes from the north, and returning by the same troubled path. But return they did, and others after them, until we came in time to know that those whom we feared had left all the lands of light to dwell in the Mouth, where—they said—the waters at times possessed a quality magical and ineffable. They spoke of the third age, and the second and the first—all these, they said, had returned not in the meat, but in the waters of the Mouth. With these avowals they taunted us, flinging at us jagged stones fallen from the Teeth. But we saw that, however fierce, they were few; and when we questioned them, shouting from a distance, they would not reply.

It was at this time that Deepdelver's woman Singing was stolen by a Man of the Face, and into those times I was born—yes, I saw them, with these same eyes that behold you now, remembering them in the time I was a child.

Deepdelver was not stronger than other men, nor swifter; and others there were who were cleverer than he. Why then was he counted a hero when they were not? This was the question I put to my parents; and the answer they gave was that he had done a wonderful thing, going to Everdark to bring back the woman he loved; but that reply was no answer—would any other, stronger, swifter, more cunning, not have done as Deepdelver had? No. There was in him something better than strength or cunning, that which made him go forward and not back. This it was that made Deepdelver a hero, that brought him into Everdark, and to the light again alive.

As to Singing, what can an old man say? Her beauty cursed me, if you will, though I was then but a little child. I have never seen another and never shall—she ennobled us all; wherever she stood was for that time a place of peace and beauty. Of the crime that befell her I was then too young to know, but I give it as I received it.

With others of her age and a guard of men, of whom Deepdelver, then called by another, lesser, name, was one, she journeyed to the Eyes to bathe. Now at that time men no longer went into the haunted Hair to reach the lakes from the north. But not yet were they so bold as to come too near the corners of the Mouth—no, the accepted path, then deemed safe, was to skirt the southernmost spinney of the Hair, near the Ear, and thence to climb to the Eyes by an oblique ascent.

Now this party of young men and maidens were so doing when there came upon them such a calamity as we, of this latter age, have so much more knowledge than they. An overflow from the nearer lake, forming itself into a great mass of water, came hurtling down on them; and they scattered—none looking to the others, but each fleeing in that direction that seemed to him easiest. Now it so happened that Singing's path led her to the Mouth.

When the Tear had passed the young men and maids joined again, laughing and each telling their tale of escape until, as they reckoned their numbers, their laughter hushed. Wide they quested then for Singing, but not to the Mouth until with the passing of time it grew upon them that if Singing had not, indeed, been washed away, then it was there that they must search for her. None spoke this knowledge, but it waxed among them; and at length they would not look at one another for the shame of it—but already Deepdelver was gone.

No one had he told of his plan, going alone to the very precipices of the Lips, and from those dark, ill-omened heights, staring, alone, at the Teeth themselves, the dread portals of the sunless realm, found within him the strength to enter there; such a man is not like us, though he walk among us; the ghosts who wander forever through the Hair might, if they saw a living man walking unafraid where they are accustomed to take such ease as is permitted the Dead, believe him to be a ghost even as they: but— if we are not all specters now—it would not be so, because he would have life in him. Just so such men as you and I, seeing a Deepdelver, think him but our peer.

Often I questioned him—young as I was, and shameless—of what he found within the Teeth, and the rescue of Singing. Little would he tell me. There are watery caves beneath the Tongue, by his saying. There he swam in halflight through waves clearer, yet thicker, than those of the lakes; and met a gentle race who begged him to go no farther, offering in the stead of Singing milk-pale maidens, languid, gentle, and enamoured of love, whom he spurned.

We call ourselves the People of the Neck, but who but Deepdelver ever knew the extent of that kingdom; who but he ever, in the long song of history, went down the Throat? That road he took, leaving the last of the light. Savages he met there, and, defeating their chief in solitary combat, bound him when his vassels fled—till hunger forced from him the tale of Singing's passing, and her captor's. Deeper they had gone by his telling, and even Deepdelver's mighty strength—so he himself recounted it —died within him.

Then came a wetting, but not as we have known them. The dim rills of the Throat turned to black as the waters multiplied, and there came upon Deepdelver, in the rushing confusion of those waters, all the thoughts that men have ever felt, so that he knew himself to be brave and afraid, happy yet sorrowful, God and nothing—all at once and without causes; and though his thought told him that to do so was death, he dived into the waters and swam with them, laughing to die so, laughing in the breakers, dizzy with delight in the darkness, knowing that it was death but eager to die so.

So he came to the depths, to Everdark, and heard there the weeping of Singing. Who can tell a tale that was born in the blackness? How he found her and killed her captor, drowning him, though he was himself delirious, in the millrace of madness. How the Inner People won them, they who then ate what they had from the waters, those unseen ones who never stand in sun, whelming Deepdelver in their myriads; how he their slave taught them to tear the meat they trod and so live lawfully, and how they gave freedom to him, and Singing too, when once they had tasted; how the two made their way midst difficulties and dangers to the Neck again; all these are more than I can say. But you must know the courage, and the history of your People before you fare forth; and I have told you.

Field and hill are cold now, and the World itself dying or dead, and the lands are filled with ghouls. It is time you go.

This was the last story.

Ship-Sister, Star-Sister

ROBERT SILVERBERG

SIXTEEN LIGHT-YEARS from Earth today, in the fifth month of the voyage, and the silent throb of acceleration continues to drive the velocity higher. Three games of *go* are in progress in the ship's lounge. The year-captain stands at the entrance to the lounge, casually watching the players: Roy and Sylvia, Leon and Chiang, Heinz and Elliot. *Go* has been a craze aboard ship for weeks. The players—some eighteen or twenty members of the expedition have caught the addiction by now—sit hour after hour, contemplating strategies, devising variations, grasping the smooth black or white stones between forefinger and second finger, putting the stones down against the wooden board with the proper smart sharp clacking sound. The year-captain himself does not play, though the game once interested him to the point of obsession, long ago; he finds his responsibilities so draining that an exercise in simulated territorial conquest does not attract him now. He comes here often to watch, however, remaining five or ten minutes, then going on about his duties.

The best of the players is Roy, the mathematician, a large, heavy man with a soft sleepy face. He sits with his eyes closed, awaiting in tranquility his turn to play. "I am purging myself of the need to win," he told the year-captain yesterday when asked what occupies his mind while he waits. Purged or not, Roy wins more than half of his games, even though he gives most of his opponents a handicap of four or five stones.

He gives Sylvia a handicap of only two. She is a delicate woman, fine-boned and shy, a geneticist, and she plays well although slowly. She makes her move. At the sound of it Roy opens his eyes. He studies the board, points, and says, "*Atari,*" the conventional way of calling to his opponent's attention the fact that her move will enable him to capture several of her stones. Sylvia laughs lightly and retracts her move. After a moment she moves again. Roy nods and picks up a white stone, which he holds for nearly a minute before he places it.

The year-captain would like to speak with Sylvia about one of her experiments, but he sees she will be occupied with the game for another hour or more. The conversation can wait. No one hurries aboard this ship. They have plenty of time for everything: a lifetime, maybe, if no habitable planet can be found. The universe is theirs. He scans the board and tries to anticipate Sylvia's next move. Soft footsteps sound behind him. The year-captain turns. Noelle, the ship's communicator, is approaching the lounge. She is a slim, sightless girl with long, dark hair, and she customarily walks the corridors unaided: no sensors for her, not even a cane. Occasionally she stumbles, but usually her balance is excellent and her sense of the location of obstacles is superb. It is a kind of arrogance for the blind to shun assistance, perhaps. But also it is a kind of desperate poetry.

As she comes up to him she says, "Good morning, year-captain."

Noelle is infallible in making such identifications. She claims to be able to distinguish members of the expedition by the tiny characteristic sounds they make: their patterns of breathing, their coughs, the rustling of their clothing. Among the others there is some skepticism about this. Many aboard the ship believe that Noelle is reading their minds. She does not deny that she possesses the power of telepathy; but she insists that the only mind to which she has direct access is that of her twin sister Yvonne, far away on Earth.

He turns to her. His eyes meet hers: an automatic act, a habit. Hers, dark and clear, stare disconcertingly through his forehead. He says, "I'll have a report for you to transmit in about two hours."

"I'm ready whenever." She smiles faintly. She listens a moment to the clacking of the *go* stones. "Three games being played?" she asks.

"Yes."

"How strange that the game hasn't begun to lose its hold on them by this time."

"Its grip is powerful," the year-captain says.

"It must be. How good it is to be able to give yourself so completely to a game."

"I wonder. Playing *go* consumes a great deal of valuable time."

"Time?" Noelle laughs. "What is there to do with time, except to consume it?" After a moment she says, "Is it a difficult game?"

"The rules are quite simple. The application of the rules is another matter entirely. It's a deeper and more subtle game than chess, I think."

Her blank eyes wander across his face and suddenly lock into his. "How long would it take for me to learn how to play?"

"You?"

"Why not? I also need amusement, year-captain."

"The board has hundreds of intersections. Moves may be made at any of them. The patterns formed are complex and constantly changing. Someone who is unable to see—"

"My memory is excellent," Noelle says. "I can visualize the board and make the necessary corrections as play proceeds. You need only tell me where you put down your stones. And guide my hand, I suppose, when I make my moves."

"I doubt that it'll work, Noelle."

"Will you teach me anyway?"

The ship is sleek, tapered, graceful: a silver bullet streaking across the universe at a velocity that has at this point come to exceed a million kilometers per second. No. In fact the ship is no bullet at all, but rather something squat and awkward, as clumsy as any ordinary spacegoing vessel, with an elaborate spidery superstructure of extensor arms and antennae and observation booms and other externals. Yet the year-captain persists in thinking of it as sleek and tapered and graceful, because of its incredible speed. It carries him without friction through the vast empty gray cloak of nospace at a velocity greater than that of light. He knows better, but he is unable to shake that streamlined image from his mind.

Already the expedition is sixteen light-years from Earth. That isn't an easy thing for him to grasp. He feels the force of it, but not the true meaning. He can tell himself, *Already we are sixteen kilometers from home,* and understand that readily enough. *Already we are sixteen hundred kilometers from home,* yes, he can understand that too. What about *Already we are sixteen million kilometers from home?* That much strains comprehension—a gulf, a gulf, a terrible empty dark gulf—but he thinks he is able to understand even so great a distance, after a fashion. Sixteen light-years, though? How can he explain that to himself? Brilliant stars flank the tube of nospace through which the ship now travels, and he knows that his gray-flecked beard will have turned entirely white before the light of those stars glitters in the night sky of Earth. Yet only a few months have elapsed since the departure of the expedition. How miraculous it is, he thinks, to have come so far, so swiftly.

Even so, there is a greater miracle. He will ask Noelle to relay a message to Earth an hour after lunch, and he knows that he will have an acknowledgment from Control Central in Brazil before dinner. That seems an even greater miracle to him.

Her cabin is neat, austere, underfurnished: no paintings, no light-sculptures, nothing to please the visual sense, only a few small sleek bronze statuettes, a smooth oval slab of green stone, and some objects evidently chosen for their rich textures—a strip of nubby fabric stretched across a frame, a sea-urchin's stony test, a collection of rough sandstone chunks. Everything is meticulously arranged. Does someone help her keep the place tidy? She moves serenely from point to point in the little room, never in danger of a collision; her confidence of motion is unnerving to the year-captain, who sits patiently waiting for her to settle down. She is pale, precisely groomed, her dark hair drawn tightly back from her forehead and held by an intricate ivory clasp. Her lips are full, her nose is rounded. She wears a soft flowing robe. Her body is attractive: he has seen her in the baths and knows of her high full breasts, her ample curving hips, her creamy perfect skin. Yet so far as he has heard she has had no shipboard liaisons. Is it because she is blind? Perhaps one tends not to think of a blind person as a potential sexual partner. Why should that be? Maybe because one hesitates to take advantage of a blind person in a sexual encounter, he suggests, and immediately catches himself up, startled, wondering why he should think of any sort of sexual relationship as *taking advantage*. Well, then, possibly compassion for her handicap gets in the way of erotic feeling; pity too easily becomes patronizing, and kills desire. He rejects that theory: glib, implausible. Could it be that people fear to approach her, suspecting that she is able to read their inmost thoughts? She has repeatedly denied any ability to enter minds other than her sister's. Besides, if you have nothing to hide, why be put off by her telepathy? No, it must be something else, and now he thinks he has isolated it: that Noelle is so self-contained, so serene, so much wrapped up in her blindness and her mind-power and her unfathomable communion with her distant sister that no one dares to breach the crystalline barricades that guard her inner self. She is unapproached because she seems unapproachable; her strange perfection of soul sequesters her, keeping others at a distance the way extraordinary physical beauty can sometimes keep people at a distance. She does not arouse desire because she does not seem at all human. She gleams. She is a flawless machine, an integral part of the ship.

He unfolds the text of today's report to Earth. "Not that there's anything new to tell them," he says, "but I suppose we have to file the daily communique all the same."

"It would be cruel if we didn't. We mean so much to them."

"I wonder."

"Oh, yes. Yvonne says they take our messages from her as fast as they come in, and send them out on every channel. Word from us is terribly important to them."

"As a diversion, nothing more. As the latest curiosity. Intrepid explorers venturing into the uncharted wilds of interstellar nospace." His voice sounds harsh to him, his rhythms of speech coarse and blurting. His words surprise him. He had not known he felt this way about Earth. Still, he goes on. "That's all we represent: novelty, vicarious adventure, a moment of amusement."

"Do you mean that? It sounds so awful cynical."

He shrugs. "Another six months and they'll be completely bored with us and our communiques. Perhaps sooner than that. A year and they'll have forgotten us."

She says, "I don't see you as a cynical man. Yet you often say such—" She falters. "Such—"

"Such blunt things? I'm a realist, I guess. Is that the same as a cynic?"

"Don't try to label yourself, year-captain."

"I only try to look at things realistically."

"You don't know what real is. You don't know what you are, year-captain."

The conversation is suddenly out of control: much too charged, much too intimate. She has never spoken like this before. It is as if there is a malign electricity in the air, a prickly field that distorts their normal selves, making them unnaturally tense and aggressive. He feels panic. If he disturbs the delicate balance of Noelle's consciousness, will she still be able to make contact with far-off Yvonne?

He is unable to prevent himself from parrying: "Do *you* know what I am, then?"

She tells him, "You're a man in search of himself. That's why you volunteered to come all the way out here."

"And why did you volunteer to come all the way out here, Noelle?" he asks helplessly.

She lets the lids slide slowly down over her unseeing eyes and offers no reply. He tries to salvage things a bit by saying more calmly into her tense silence, "Never mind. I didn't intend to upset you. Shall we transmit the report?"

"Wait."

"All right."

She appears to be collecting herself. After a moment she says, less edgily, "How do you think they see us at home? As ordinary human beings doing an unusual job or as superhuman creatures engaged in an epic voyage?"

"Right now, as superhuman creatures, epic voyage."

"And later we'll become more ordinary in their eyes?"

"Later we'll become nothing to them. They'll forget us."

"How sad." Her tone tingles with a grace-note of irony. She may be laughing at him. "And you, year-captain? Do you picture yourself as ordinary or as superhuman?"

"Something in between. Rather more than ordinary, but no demigod."

"I regard myself as quite ordinary except in two respects," she says sweetly.

"One is your telepathic communion with your sister and the other—" He hesitates, mysteriously uncomfortable at naming it. "The other is your blindness."

"Of course," she says. Smiles. Radiantly. "Shall we do the report now?"

"Have you made contact with Yvonne?"

"Yes. She's waiting."

"Very well, then." Glancing at his notes, he begins slowly to read: "Shipday 117. Velocity. . . . Apparent location. . . ."

She naps after every transmission. They exhaust her. She was beginning to fade even before he reached the end of today's message; now, as he steps into the corridor, he knows she will be asleep before he closes the door. He leaves, frowning, troubled by the odd outburst of tension between them and by his mysterious attack of "realism." By what right does he say Earth will grow jaded with the voyagers? All during the years of preparation for this first interstellar journey the public excitement never flagged, indeed spurred the voyagers themselves on at times when their interminable training routines threatened *them* with boredom. Earth's messages, relayed by Yvonne to Noelle, vibrate with eager queries; the curiosity of the homeworld has been overwhelming since the start. Tell us, tell us, tell us!

But there is so little to tell, really, except in that one transcendental area where there is so much. And how, really, can any of that be told?

How can *this*—

He pauses by the viewplate in the main transit corridor, a rectangular window a dozen meters long that gives direct access to the external environment. The pearl-gray emptiness of nospace, dense and pervasive, presses tight against the skin of the ship. During the training period

the members of the expedition had been warned to anticipate nothing in the way of outside inputs as they crossed
the galaxy; they would be shuttling through a void of infinite length, a matter-free tube, and there would be no
sights to entertain them, no backdrop of remote nebulas,
no glittering stars, no stray meteors, not so much as a
pair of colliding atoms yielding the tiniest momentary
spark, only an eternal sameness, like a blank wall. They
had been taught methods of coping with that: turn in-
ward, demand no delights from the universe beyond the
ship, make the ship itself your universe. And yet, and yet,
how misguided those warnings had been! Nospace was
not a wall but rather a window. It was impossible for
those on Earth to understand what revelations lay in that
seeming emptiness. The year-captain, head throbbing
from his encounter with Noelle, now revels in his keen-
est pleasure. A glance at the viewplate reveals that place
where the immanent becomes the transcendent: the year-
captain sees once again the infinite reverberating waves
of energy that sweep through the grayness. What lies
beyond the ship is neither a blank wall nor an empty
tube; it is a stunning profusion of interlocking energy
fields, linking everything to everything, it is music that
also is light, it is light that also is music, and those aboard
the ship are sentient particles wholly enmeshed in that
vast all-engulfing reverberation, that radiant song of
gladness, that is the universe. The voyagers journey joy-
ously toward the center of all things, giving themselves
gladly into the care of cosmic forces far surpassing human control and understanding. He presses his hands
against the cool glass. He puts his face close to it. *What
do I see, what do I feel, what am I experiencing?* It is
instant revelation, every time. It is—almost, *almost!*—the
sought-after oneness. Barriers remain, but yet he is aware
of an altered sense of space and time, a knowledge of the
awesome something that lurks in the vacancies between
the spokes of the cosmos, something majestic and powerful; he knows that that something is part of himself, and

he is part of it. When he stands at the viewplate he yearns to open the ship's great hatch and tumble into the eternal. But not yet, not yet. Barriers remain. The voyage has only begun. They grow closer every day to that which they seek, but the voyage has only begun.

How could we convey any of this to those who remain behind? How could we make them understand?

Not with words. Never with words.

Let them come out here and see for themselves—

He smiles. He trembles and does a little shivering wriggle of delight. He turns away from the viewplate, drained, ecstatic.

Noelle lies in uneasy dreams. She is aboard a ship, an archaic three-master struggling in an icy sea. The rigging sparkles with fierce icicles, which now and again snap free in the cruel gales and smash with little tinkling sounds against the deck. The deck wears a slippery, shiny coating of thin hard ice, and footing is treacherous. Great eroded bergs heave wildly in the gray water, rising, slapping the waves, subsiding. If one of those bergs hits the hull, the ship will sink. So far they have been lucky about that, but now a more subtle menace is upon them. The sea is freezing over. It congeals, coagulates, becomes a viscous fluid, surging sluggishly. Broad glossy plaques toss on the waves: new ice-floes, colliding, grinding, churning; the floes are at war, destroying one another's edges, but some are making treaties, uniting to form a single implacable shield. When the sea freezes altogether the ship will be crushed. And now it is freezing. The ship can barely make headway. The sails belly out uselessly, straining at their lines. The wind makes a lyre out of the rigging as the ice-coated ropes twang and sing. The hull creaks like an old man; the grip of the ice is heavy. The timbers are yielding. The end is near. They will all perish. They will all perish. Noelle emerges from her cabin, goes above, seizes the railing, sways, prays, wonders when the wind's fist will punch through the stiff, frozen canvas of the sails. Nothing can save them. But now! Yes, yes! A glow overhead! Yvonne, Yvonne! She comes. She hovers like a goddess in the black star-pocked sky. Soft golden light streams from her. She is smiling, and her smile thaws the sea. The ice relents. The air grows gentle. The ship is freed. It sails on, unhindered, toward the perfumed tropics.

In late afternoon Noelle drifts silently, wraith-like, into the control room where the year-captain is at work; she looks so weary and drawn that she is almost translucent; she seems unusually vulnerable, as though a harsh sound would shatter her. She has brought the year-captain Earth's answer to this morning's transmission. He takes from her the small, clear data-cube on which she has recorded her latest conversation with her sister. As Yvonne speaks in her mind, Noelle repeats the message aloud into a sensor disk, and it is captured on the cube. He wonders why she looks so wan. "Is anything wrong?" he asks. She tells him that she had had some difficulty receiving the message; the signal from Earth was strangely fuzzy. She is perturbed by that.

"It was like static," she says.

"Mental static?"

She is puzzled. Yvonne's tone is always pure, crystalline, wholly undistorted. Noelle has never had an experience like this before.

"Perhaps you were tired," he suggests. "Or maybe she was."

He fits the cube into the playback slot, and Noelle's voice comes from the speakers. She sounds unfamiliar, strained and ill at ease; she fumbles words frequently and often asks Yvonne to repeat. The message, what he can make out of it, the usual cheery stuff, predigested news from the homeworld—politics, sports, the planetary weather, word of the arts and sciences, special greetings for three or four members of the expedition, expressions of general good wishes—everything light, shallow, amiable. The static disturbs him. What if the telepathic link should fail? What if they were to lose contact with Earth altogether? He asks himself why that should trouble him so. The ship is self-sufficient; it needs no guidance from Earth in order to function properly, nor do the voyagers really have to have daily information about events on the mother planet. Then why care if silence descends? Why not accept the fact that they are no longer Earthbound in any way, that they have become virtually a new species as they leap, faster than light, outward into the stars? No. He cares. The link matters. He decides that it has to do with what they are experiencing in relation to the intense throbbing grayness outside, that interchange of energies, that growing sense of universal connection. They are making discoveries every day, not astronomical but —well, spiritual—and, the year-captain thinks, what a pity if none of this can ever be communicated to those who have remained behind. We must keep the link open.

"Maybe," he says, "we ought to let you and Yvonne rest for a few days."

They look upon me as some sort of nun because I'm blind and special. I hate that but there's nothing I can do to change it. I am what they think I am. I lie awake imagining men touching my body. The year-captain stands over me. I see his face clearly, the skin flushed and sweaty, the eyes gleaming. He strokes my breasts. He put his lips to my lips. Suddenly, terribly, he embraces me and I scream. Why do I scream?

"You promised to teach me how to play," she says, pouting a little. They are in the ship's lounge. Four games are under way: Elliot and Sylvia, Roy and Paco, David and Heinz, Mike and Bruce. Her pout fascinates him: such a little-girl gesture, so charming, so human. She seems to be in much better shape today, even though there was trouble again in the transmission. Yvonne complaining that the morning report was coming through indistinctly and noisily. Noelle has decided that the noise is some sort of local phenomenon, something like a sunspot effect, and will vanish once they are far enough from this sector of nospace. He is not as sure of this as she is, but she probably has a better understanding of such things than he. "Teach me, year-captain," she prods. "I really do want to know how to play. Have faith in me."

"All right," he says. The game may prove valuable to her, a relaxing pastime, a timely distraction. "This is the board. It has 19 horizontal lines, 19 vertical lines. The stones are played on the intersections of these lines, not on the squares that they form." He takes her hand and traces, with the tips of her fingers, the pattern of intersecting lines. They have been printed with a thick ink, easily discernible against the flatness of the board. "These nine dots are called stars," he tells her. "They serve as orientation points." He touches her fingertips to the nine stars. "We give the lines in this direction numbers, from 1 to 19, and we give the lines in the other direction letters, from A to T, leaving out I. Thus we can identify positions on the board. This is B10, this is D18, this is J4, do you follow?" He feels despair. How can she ever commit the board to memory? But she looks untroubled as she runs her hand along the edges of the board, murmuring, "A, B, C, D. . . ."

The other games have halted. Everyone in the lounge is watching them. He guides her hand toward the two trays of stones, the white and the black, and shows her the traditional way of picking up a stone between two fingers and clapping it down against the board. "The stronger player uses the white stones," he says. "Black always moves first. The players take turns placing stones, one at a time, on any unoccupied intersection. Once a stone is placed it is never moved unless it is captured, when it is removed at once from the board."

"And the purpose of the game?" she asks.

"To control the largest possible area with the smallest possible number of stones. You build walls. The score is reckoned by counting the number of vacant intersections within your walls, plus the number of prisoners you have taken." Methodically he explains the technique of play to her: the placing of stones, the seizure of territory, the capture of opposing stones. He illustrates by setting up simulated situations on the board, calling out the location of each stone as he places it: "Black holds P12, Q12, R12, S12, T12, and also P11, P10, P9, Q8, R8, S8, T8. White holds—" Somehow she visualizes the positions; she repeats the patterns after him, and asks questions that show she sees the board clearly in her mind. Within twenty minutes she understands the basic ploys. Several times, in describing maneuvers to her, he gives her an incorrect coordinate—the board, after all, is not marked with numbers and letters, and he misgauges the points occasionally—but each time she corrects him, gently saying, "N13? Don't you mean N12?"

At length she says, "I think I follow everything now. Would you like to play a game?"

Consider your situation carefully. You are twenty years old, female, sightless. You have never married or even entered into a basic pairing. Your only real human contact is with your twin sister, who is like yourself blind and single. Her mind is fully open to yours. Yours is to hers. You and she are two halves of one soul, inexplicably embedded in separate bodies. With her, only with her, do you feel complete. Now you are asked to take part in a voyage to the stars, without her, a voyage that is sure to cut you off from her forever. You are told that if you leave Earth aboard the starship there is no chance that you will ever see your sister again. You are told, also, that your presence is important to the success of the voyage, for without your help it would take decades or even centuries for news of the starship to reach Earth, but if you are aboard it will be possible to maintain instantaneous communication across any distance. What should you do? Consider. Consider.

You consider. And you volunteer to go, of course. You are needed: how can you refuse? As for your sister, you will naturally lose the opportunity to touch her, to hold her close, to derive direct comfort from her presence. Otherwise you will lose nothing. Never "see" her again? No. You can "see" her just as well, certainly, from a distance of a million light-years as you can from the next room. There can be no doubt of that.

The morning transmission. Noelle, sitting with her back to the year-captain, listens to what he reads her and sends it coursing over a gap of more than sixteen light-years. "Wait," she says. "Yvonne is calling for a repeat. From 'metabolic.'" He pauses, goes back, reads again: "*Metabolic balances remain normal, although, as earlier reported, some of the older members of the expedition have begun to show trace deficiencies of manganese and potassium. We are taking appropriate corrective steps, and—*" Noelle halts him with a brusque gesture. He waits, and she bends forward, forehead against the table, hands pressed tightly to her temples. "Static again," she says. "It's worse today."

"Are you getting through at all?"

"I'm getting through, yes. But I have to push, to push, to push. And still Yvonne asks for repeats. I don't know what's happening, year-captain."

"The distance—"

"No!"

"Better than sixteen light-years."

"No," she says. "We've already demonstrated that distance effects aren't a factor. If there's no falling-off of signal after a million kilometers, after one light-year, after ten light-years, no perceptible drop in clarity and accuracy whatever, then there shouldn't be any qualitative diminution suddenly at sixteen light-years. Don't you think I've thought about this?"

"Noelle—"

"Attenuation of signal is one thing, and interference is another. An attenuation curve is a gradual slope. Yvonne and I have had perfect contact from the day we left Earth until just a few days ago. And now—no, year-captain, it can't be attenuation. It has to be some sort of interference. A local effect."

"Yes, like sunspots, I know. But—"

"Let's start again. Yvonne's calling for signal. Go on from '*manganese and potassium.*' "

"*—manganese and potassium. We are taking appropriate corrective steps—*"

Playing *go* seems to ease her tension. He has not played in years, and he is rusty at first, but within minutes the old associations return and he finds himself setting up chains of stones with skill. Although he expects her to play poorly, unable to remember the patterns on the board after the first few moves, she proves to have no difficulty keeping the entire array in her mind. Only in one respect has she overestimated herself: for all her precision of coordination, she is unable to place the stones exactly, tending rather to disturb the stones already on the board as she makes her moves. After a little while she admits failure and thenceforth she calls out the plays she desires —M17, Q6, P6, R4, C11—and he places the stones for her. In the beginning he plays unaggressively, assuming that as a novice she will be haphazard and weak, but soon he discovers that she is adroitly expanding and protecting her territory while pressing a sharp attack against his, and he begins to devise more cunning strategies. They play for two hours and he wins by 16 points, a comfortable margin but nothing to boast about, considering that he is an experienced and adept player and that this is her first game.

The others are skeptical of her instant ability. "Sure she plays well," Heinz mutters. "She's reading your mind, isn't she? She can see the board through your eyes and she knows what you're planning."

"The only mind open to her is her sister's," the year-captain says vehemently.

"How can you be sure she's telling the truth?"

The year-captain scowls. "Play a game with her yourself. You'll see whether it's skill or mind-reading that's at work."

Heinz, looking sullen, agrees. That evening he challenges Noelle; later he comes to the year-captain, abashed. "She plays well. She almost beat me, and she did it fairly."

The year-captain plays a second game with her. She sits almost motionless, eyes closed, lips compressed, offering the coordinates of her moves in a quiet bland monotone, like some sort of game-playing mechanism. She rarely takes long to decide on a move and she makes no blunders that must be retracted. Her capacity to devise game-patterns has grown astonishingly; she nearly shuts him off from the center, but he recovers the initiative and manages a narrow victory. Afterward she loses once more to Heinz, but again she displays an increase of ability, and in the evening she defeats Chiang, a respected player. Now she becomes invincible. Undertaking two or three matches every day, she triumphs over Heinz, Sylvia, the year-captain, and Leon; go has become something immense to her, something much more than a mere game, a simple test of strength; she focuses her energy on the board so intensely that her playing approaches the level of a religious discipline, a kind of meditation. On the fourth day she defeats Roy, the ship's champion, with such economy that everyone is dazzled. Roy can speak of nothing else. He demands a rematch and is defeated again.

Noelle wondered, as the ship was lifting from Earth, whether she really would be able to maintain contact with Yvonne across the vast span of interstellar space. She had nothing but faith to support her belief that the power that joined their minds was wholly unaffected by distance. They had often spoken to each other without difficulty from opposite sides of the planet, yes, but would it be so simple when they were half a galaxy apart? During the early hours of the voyage she and Yvonne kept up a virtually continuous linking, and the signal remained clear and sharp, with no perceptible falling off of reception, as the ship headed outward. Past the orbit of the moon, past the million-kilometer mark, past the orbit of Mars: clear and sharp, clear and sharp. They had passed the first test: clarity of signal was not a quantitative function of distance. But Noelle remained unsure of what would happen once the ship abandoned conventional power and shunted into nospace in order to attain faster-than-light velocity. She would then be in a space apart from Yvonne; in effect she would be in another universe; would she still be able to reach her sister's mind? Tension rose in her as the moment of the shunt approached, for she had no idea what life would be like for her in the absence of Yvonne. To face that dreadful silence, to find herself thrust into such terrible isolation—but it did not happen. They entered nospace and her awareness of Yvonne never flickered. *Here we are, wherever we are*, she said, and moments later came Yvonne's response, a cheery greeting from the old continuum. Clear and sharp, clear and sharp. Nor did the signal grow more tenuous in the weeks that followed. Clear and sharp, clear and sharp, until the static began.

The year-captain visualizes the contact between the two sisters as an arrow whistling from star to star, as fire speeding through a shining tube, as a river of pure force coursing down a celestial waveguide. He sees the joining of those two minds as a stream of pure light binding the moving ship to the far-off mother world. Sometimes he dreams of Yvonne and Noelle, Noelle and Yvonne, and the glowing bond that stretches between the sisters gives off so brilliant a radiance that he stirs and moans and presses his forehead into the pillow.

The interference grows worse. Neither Noelle nor Yvonne can explain what is happening; Noelle clings, without conviction, to her sunspot analogy. They still manage to make contact twice daily, but it is increasingly a strain on the sisters' resources, for every sentence must be repeated two or three times, and whole blocks of words now do not get through at all. Noelle has become thin and haggard. *Go* refreshes her, or at least diverts her from this failing of her powers. She has become a master of the game, awarding even Roy a two-stone handicap; although she occasionally loses, her play is always distinguished, extraordinarily original in its sweep and design. When she is not playing she tends to be remote and aloof. She is in all aspects a more elusive person than she was before the onset of this communications crisis.

Noelle dreams that her blindness has been taken from her. Sudden light surrounds her, and she opens her eyes, sits up, looks about in awe and wonder, saying to herself, this is a table, this is a chair, this is how my statuettes look, this is what my sea urchin is like. She is amazed by the beauty of everything in her room. She rises, goes forward, stumbling at first, groping, then magically gaining poise and balance, learning how to walk in this new way, judging the positions of things not by echoes and air currents but rather by using her eyes. Information floods her. She moves about the ship, discovering the faces of her shipmates. You are Roy, you are Sylvia, you are Heinz, you are the year-captain. They look, surprisingly, very much as she had imagined them: Roy fleshy and red-faced, Sylvia fragile, the year-captain lean and fierce, Heinz like this, Elliot like that, everyone matching expectations. Everyone beautiful. She goes to the window of which the others all talk, and looks out into the famous grayness. Yes, yes, it is as they say it is: a cosmos of wonders, a miracle of complex pulsating tones, level after level of incandescent reverberation sweeping outward toward the rim of the boundless universe. For an hour she stands before that dense burst of rippling energies, giving herself to it and taking it into herself, and then, and then, just as the ultimate moment of illumination is coming over her, she realizes that something is wrong. Yvonne is not with her. She reaches out and does not reach Yvonne. She has somehow traded her power for the gift of sight. Yvonne? Yvonne? All is still. Where is Yvonne? Yvonne is not with her. This is only a dream, Noelle tells herself, and I will soon awaken. But she cannot awaken. In terror she cries out. It's all right, Yvonne whispers. I'm here, love, I'm here, I'm here, just as always. Yes. Noelle feels the closeness. Trembling, she embraces her sister. Looks at her. I can see, Yvonne! I can see! Noelle realizes that in her first rapture she quite forgot to look at herself, though she rushed about looking at everything else. Mirrors have never been part of her world. She looks at Yvonne, which is like looking at herself, and Yvonne is beautiful, her hair dark and silken and lustrous, her face smooth and pale, her features fine of outline, her eyes— her blind eyes—alive and sparkling. Noelle tells Yvonne how beautiful she is, and Yvonne nods, and they laugh and hold one another close, and they begin to weep with pleasure and love, and Noelle awakens, and the world is dark around her.

"I have the day's report," the year-captain says wearily. "Do you feel like trying again?"

"Of course I do." She gives him a ferocious smile. "Don't even hint at giving up, year-captain. We're going to find some way to get around this interference."

"I hope you're right." He rustles his papers. "Okay. Let's go, Noelle. Shipday 128. Velocity. . . ."

"Give me another moment to get ready," Noelle says.

He falls silent. She closes her eyes and prepares to send. She is conscious, as ever, of the presence of Yvonne. Even when no specific information is flowing between them, there is perpetual contact, there is the sense of the other's being near, that warm proprioceptive awareness such as one has of one's own arm or leg or lip. But between that impalpable subliminal contact and the transmission of specific content must come several steps. Yvonne and Noelle are human biopsychic resonators constituting a communications network; there is a tuning procedure for them as for any transmitters and receivers. Noelle opens herself to the radiant energy spectrum, vibratory, pulsating, that will carry her message to her Earthbound sister. As the transmitting circuit in this interchange she must be the one to attain maximum energy flow. Quickly, intuitively, she activates her own energy centers, the one in the spine, the one in the solar plexus, the one at the top of the skull; energy pours from her and instantaneously spans the galaxy. But today there is an odd and troublesome splashback effect: monitoring the circuit, she is immediately aware that the signal has failed to reach Yvonne. Yvonne is there, Yvonne is tuned and expectant, yet something is jamming the channel and nothing gets through, not a single syllable. "The interference is worse than ever," she tells the year-captain. "I feel as if I could put my hand out and *touch* Yvonne. But she's not reading me and nothing's coming back from her." With a little shake of her shoulders Noelle alters the sending frequency; she feels a corresponding adjustment at Yvonne's end of the connection; but again they are thwarted, again there is total blockage. Her signal is going forth and is being soaked up by—what? How can such a thing happen?

Now she makes a determined effort to boost the output of the system. She addresses herself to the neural center in her spine, exciting its energies, using them to drive the next center to a more intense vibrational tone, harnessing that to push the highest center of all to its greatest harmonic capacity. Up and down the energy bands she roves. Nothing. Nothing. She shivers; she huddles; she is physically emptied by the strain. "I can't get through," she murmurs. "She's there, I can feel her there, I know she's working to read me. But I can't transmit any sort of intelligible coherent message."

Almost seventeen light-years from Earth and the only communication channel is blocked. The year-captain is overwhelmed by frosty terrors. The ship, the self-sufficient autonomous ship, has become a mere gnat blowing in a hurricane. The voyagers hurtle blindly into the depths of an unknown universe, alone, alone, alone. He was so smug about not needing any link to Earth; but now that the link is gone he shivers and cowers. Everything has been made new. There are no rules. Human beings have never been this far from home. He presses himself against the viewplate and the famous grayness just beyond, swirling and eddying, mocks him with its immensity. Leap into me, it calls, leap, leap, lose yourself in me, drown in me.

Behind him: the sound of soft footsteps. Noelle. She touches his hunched, knotted shoulders. "It's all right," she whispers. "You're over-reacting. Don't make such a tragedy out of it." But it is. Her tragedy, more than anyone's, hers and Yvonne's. But also his, theirs, everybody's. Cut off. Lost in a foggy silence.

Down in the lounge people are singing. Boisterous voices, Elliot, Chiang, Leon.

> *Travelin' Dan was a spacefarin' man*
> *He jumped in the nospace tube.*

The year-captain whirls, seizes Noelle, pulls her against him. Feels her trembling. Comforts her, where a moment before she had been comforting him. Yes, yes, yes, yes, he murmurs. With his arm around her shoulders he turns, so that both of them are facing the viewplate. As if she could see. Nospace dances and churns an inch from his nose. He feels a hot wind blowing through the ship, the khamsin, the sirocco, the simoom, the leveche, a sultry wind, a killing wind coming out of the gray strangeness, and he forces himself not to fear that wind. It is a wind of life, he tells himself, a wind of joy, a cool sweet wind, the mistral, the tramontana. Why should he think there is anything to fear in the realm beyond the viewplate? How beautiful it is out there, how ecstatically beautiful! How sad that we can never tell anyone about it, now, except one another. A strange peace unexpectedly descends on him. Everything is going to be all right, he insists. No harm will come of what has happened. And perhaps some good. And perhaps some good. Benefits lurk in the darkest places.

She plays *go* obsessively, beating everyone. She seems to live in the lounge twenty hours a day. Sometimes she takes on two opponents at once—an incredible feat, considering that she must hold the constantly changing intricacies of both boards in her memory—and defeats them both: two days after losing verbal-level contact with Yvonne, she simultaneously triumphs over Roy and Heinz before an audience of thirty. She looks animated and buoyant; the sorrow she must feel over the snapping of the link she takes care to conceal. She expresses it, the others suspect, only by her manic *go*-playing. The year-captain is one of her most frequent adversaries, taking his turn at the board in the time he would have devoted to composing and dictating the communiques for Earth. He had thought *go* was over for him years ago, but he, too, is playing obsessively now, building walls and the unassailable fortresses known as eyes. There is reassurance in the rhythmic clacking march of the black and white stones. Noelle wins every game against him. She covers the board with eyes.

Who can explain the interference? No one believes that the problem is a function of anything so obvious as distance. Noelle has been quite convincing on that score: a signal that propagates perfectly for the first sixteen light-years of a journey ought not suddenly to deteriorate. There should at least have been prior sign of attenuation, and there was no attenuation, only noise interfering with and ultimately destroying the signal. Some force is intervening between the sisters. But what can it be? The idea that it is some physical effect analogous to sunspot static, that it is the product of radiation emitted by some giant star in whose vicinity they have lately been traveling, must in the end be rejected. There is no energy interface between realspace and nospace, no opportunity for any kind of electromagnetic intrusion. That much had been amply demonstrated long before any manned voyages were undertaken. The nospace tube is an impermeable wall. Nothing that has mass or charge can leap the barrier between the universe of accepted phenomena and the cocoon of nothingness that the ship's drive mechanism has woven about them, nor can a photon get across, nor even a slippery neutrino.

Many speculations excite the voyagers. The one force that *can* cross the barrier, Roy points out, is thought: intangible, unmeasurable, limitless. What if the sector of realspace corresponding to this region of the nospace tube is inhabited by beings of powerful telepathic capacity whose transmissions, flooding out over a sphere with a radius of many light-years, are able to cross the barrier just as readily as those of Yvonne? The alien mental emanations, Roy supposes, are smothering the signal from Earth.

Heinz extends this theory into a different possibility: that the interference is caused by denizens of nospace. There is a seeming paradox in this, since it has been shown mathematically that the nospace tube must be wholly matter-free except for the ship that travels through it; otherwise a body moving at speeds faster than light would generate destructive resonances as its mass exceeds infinity. But perhaps the equations are imperfectly understood. Heinz imagines giant incorporeal beings as big as asteroids, as big as planets, masses of pure energy or even pure mental force that drift freely through the tube. These beings may be sources of biopsychic transmissions that disrupt the Yvonne-Noelle circuit, or, maybe, they are actually *feeding* on the sisters' mental output, Heinz postulates. "Angels," he calls them. It is an implausible but striking concept that fascinates everyone for several days. Whether the "angels" live within the tube as proposed by Heinz, or on some world just outside it as pictured by Roy, is unimportant at the moment; the consensus aboard ship is that the interference is the work of an alien intelligence, and that arouses wonder in all.

What to do? Leon, inclining toward Roy's hypothesis, moves that they leave nospace immediately and seek the world or worlds where the "angels" dwell. The year-captain objects, noting that the plan of the voyage obliges them to reach a distance of one hundred light-years from Earth before they begin their quest for habitable planets. Roy and Leon argue that the plan is merely a guide, arbitrarily conceived, and not received scriptural writ; they are free to depart from it if some pressing reason presents itself. Heinz, supporting the year-captain, remarks that there is no need actually to leave nospace regardless of the source of the alien transmissions; if the thoughts of these creatures can come in from beyond the tube, then Noelle's thoughts can surely go outward through the tube to them, and contact can be established without the need of deviating from the plan. After all, if the interference is the work of beings sharing the tube with them, and the voyagers seek them in vain outside the tube, it may be impossible to find them again once the ship returns to nospace. This approach seems reasonable, and the question is put to Noelle: Can you attempt to open a dialogue with these beings?

She laughs. "I make no guarantees. I've never tried to talk to angels before. But I'll try, my friends. I'll try."

BLACK (Year-Captain)	WHITE (Noelle)	Black remains on offensive through Move 89. White then breaks through weak north stones and encloses a
R16	Q4	
C4	E3	

D17	D15
E16	K17
O17	E15
H17	M17
R6	Q6
Q7	P6
R5	R4
D6	C11
K3	H3
N4	O4
N3	O3
R10	C8
O15 ...	M15 ...

major center territory. Black is unable to reply adequately and White runs a chain of stones along the 19th line. At Move 141 Black launches a hopeless attack, easily crushed by White, inside White's territory. Game ends at Move 196 after Black is faced with the cat-in-the-basket trap, by which it will lose a large group in the process of capturing one stone. Score: White 81, Black 62.

She has never done anything like this before. It seems almost an act of infidelity, this opening of her mind to something or someone who is not Yvonne. But it must be done. She extends a tenuous tendril of thought that probes like a rivulet of quicksilver. Through the wall of the ship, into the surrounding grayness, upward, outward, toward, toward—

—angels?—

Angels. Oh. Brightness. Strength. Magnetism. Yes. Awareness now of a fierce roiling mass of concentrated energy close by. A mass in motion, laying a terrible stress on the fabric of the cosmos: the angel has angular momentum. It tumbles ponderously on its colossal axis. Who would have thought an angel could be so huge? Noelle is oppressed by the shifting weight of it as it makes its slow heavy axial swing. She moves closer. Oh. She is dazzled. *Too much light! Too much power!* She draws back, overwhelmed by the intensity of the other being's output. Such a mighty mind: she feels dwarfed. If she touches it with her mind she will be destroyed. She must step down the aperture, establish some kind of transformer to shield herself against the full blast of power that comes from it. It requires time and discipline. She works steadily, making adjustments, mastering new techniques, discovering capacities she had not known she possessed. And now. Yes. Try again. Slowly, slowly, slowly, with utmost care. Outward goes the tendril.

Yes.

Approaching the angel.

See? Here am I. Noelle. Noelle. Noelle. I come to you in love and fear. Touch me lightly. Just touch me—

Just a touch—

Touch—

Oh. Oh.

I see you. The light—eye of crystal—fountains of lava —oh, the light—your light—I see—I see—

Oh, like a god—

—and Semele wished to behold Zeus in all his brightness, and Zeus would have discouraged her; but Semele insisted and Zeus who loved her could not refuse her; so Zeus came upon her in full majesty and Semele was consumed by his glory, so that only the ashes of her remained, but the son she had conceived by Zeus, the boy Dionysus, was not destroyed, and Zeus saved Dionysus and took him away sealed in his thigh, bringing him forth afterward and bestowing godhood upon him—

—oh God I am Semele—

She withdraws again. Rests, regroups her powers. The force of this being is frightening. But there are ways of insulating herself against destruction, of letting the overflow of energy dissipate itself. She will try once more. She knows she stands at the brink of wonders. Now. Now. The questing mind reaches forth.

I am Noelle. I come to you in love, angel.

Contact.

The universe is burning. Bursts of wild silver light streak across the metal dome of the sky. Words turn to ash. Walls smoulder and burst into flames. There is contact. A dancing solar flare—a stream of liquid fire—a flood-tide of brilliant radiance, irresistible, unendurable, running into her, sweeping over her, penetrating her. Light everywhere.

—*Semele.*

The angel smiles and she quakes. *Open to me*, cries the vast tolling voice, and she opens and the force enters fully, sweeping through her

optic chiasma
sylvian fissure
medulla oblongata

thalamus
hypothalamus
limbic system
retricular system

pons varolii
corpus callosum
cuneus
cingulate gyrus

cingulate sulcus
orbital gyri
caudate nucleus

— c e r e b r u m ! —

claustrum
putamen
chloroid glomus

operculum
fornix

medial lemniscus

— M E S E N C E P H A L O N ! —

dura mater
dural sinus
arachnoid granulation
subarachnoid space
pia mater
cerebellum
cerebellum
cerebellum

* * *

She has been in a coma for days, wandering in delirium. Troubled, fearful, the year-captain keeps a somber vigil at her bedside. Sometimes she seems to rise toward consciousness; intelligible words, even whole sentences, bubble dreamily from her lips. She talks of light, of a brilliant, unbearable white glow, of arcs of energy, of intense solar eruptions. A star holds me, she mutters. She tells him that she has been conversing with a star. How poetic, the year-captain thinks: what a lovely metaphor. Conversing with a star. But where is she, what is happening to her? Her face is flushed; her eyes move about rapidly, darting like trapped fish beneath her closed lids. Mind to mind, she whispers, the star and I, mind to mind. She begins to hum—an edgy, whining sound, climbing almost toward inaudibility, a high-frequency keening. It pains him to hear it: hard aural radiation. Then she is silent.

Her body goes rigid. A convulsion of some sort? No. She is awakening. He sees lightning-bolts of perception flashing through her quivering musculature: the galvanized frog, twitching at the end of its leads. Her eyelids tremble. She makes a little moaning noise.

She looks up at him.

The year-captain says gently, "Your eyes are open. I think you can see me now, Noelle. Your eyes are tracking me, aren't they?"

"I can see you, yes." Her voice is hesitant, faltering, strange for a moment, a foreign voice, but then it becomes more like its usual self as she asks, "How long was I away?"

"Eight ship-days. We were worried."

"You look exactly as I though you would look," she says. "Your face is hard. But not a dark face. Not a hostile face."

"Do you want to talk about where you went, Noelle?" She smiles. "I talked with the—angel."

"Angel?"

"Not really an angel, year-captain. Not a physical being, either, not any kind of alien species. More like the energy-creatures Heinz was discussing. But bigger. Bigger. I don't know what it was, year-captain."

"You told me you were talking with a star."

"—a star!"

"In your delirium. That's what you said."

Her eyes blaze with excitement. "A star! Yes! Yes, year-captain! I think I was, yes!"

"But what does that mean: talking to a star?"

She laughs. "It means talking to a star, year-captain. A great ball of fiery gas, year-captain, and it has a mind, it has a consciousness. I think that's what it was. I'm sure, now. I'm sure!"

"But how can a—"

"The light goes abruptly from her eyes. She is traveling again; she is no longer with him. He waits beside her bed. An hour, two hours, half a day. What bizarre realm has she penetrated? Her breathing is a distant, impersonal drone. So far away from him now, so remote from any place he comprehends. At last her eyelids flicker. She looks up. Her face seems transfigured. To the year-captain she still appears to be partly in that other world beyond the ship. "Yes," she says. "Not an angel, year-captain. A sun. A living intelligent sun." Her eyes are radiant. "A sun, a star, a sun," she murmurs. "I touched the consciousness of a sun. Do you believe that, year-captain? I found a network of stars that live, that think, that have minds, that have souls. That communicate. The whole universe is alive."

"A star," he says dully. "The stars have minds."

"Yes."

"All of them? Our own sun too?"

"All of them. We came to the place in the galaxy where this star lives, and it was broadcasting on my wavelength, and its output began overriding my link with Yvonne. That was the interference, year-captain. The big star, broadcasting."

This conversation has taken on for him the texture of a dream. He says quietly, "Why didn't Earth's sun override you and Yvonne when you were on Earth?"

She shrugs. "It isn't old enough. It takes—I don't know —billions of years until they're mature, until they can transmit. Our sun isn't old enough, year-captain. None of the stars close to Earth is old enough. But out here—"

"Are you in contact with it now?"

"Yes. With it and with many others. And with Yvonne."

"Yvonne too?"

"She's back in the link with me. She's in the circuit." Noelle pauses. "I can bring others into the circuit. I could bring you in, year-captain."

"Me?"

"You. Would you like to touch a star with your mind?"

"What will happen to me? Will it harm me?"

"Did it harm me, year-captain?"

"Will I still be me afterward?"

"Am I still me, year-captain?"

"I'm afraid."

"Open to me. Try. See what happens."

"I'm afraid."

"Touch a star, year-captain."

He puts his hand on hers. "Go ahead," he says, and his soul becomes a solarium.

Afterward, with the solar pulsations still reverberating in the mirrors of his mind, with blue-white sparks leaping in his synapses, he says, "What about the others?"

"I'll bring them in too."

He feels a flicker of momentary resentment. He does not want to share the illumination. But in the instant that he conceives his resentment, he abolishes it. *Let them in.*

"Take my hand," Noelle says.

They reach out together. One by one they touch the others. Roy. Sylvia. Heinz. Elliot. He feels Noelle surging in tandem with him, feels Yvonne, feels greater presences, luminous, eternal. All are joined. Ship-sister, star-sister: all become one. The year-captain realizes that the days of playing *go* have ended. They are one person; they are beyond games.

"And now," Noelle whispers. "Now we reach toward Earth. We put our strength into Yvonne, and Yvonne—"

Yvonne draws Earth's seven billion into the network.

The ship hurtles through the nospace tube. Soon the year-captain will initiate the search for a habitable planet. If they discover one, they will settle there. If not, they will go on, and it will not matter at all, and the ship and its seven billion passengers will course onward forever, warmed by the light of the friendly stars.

Harriet

STEPHEN GOLDIN and C. F. HENSEL

It BEGAN as a lovely day, with the smog level barely high enough to require nose-plugs. Rays of sulphur-colored sunlight bathed the walls of the plasticine skyscrapers and even partially illuminated the dark canyons between the buildings at street level. The neighborhood was a decent one, nice enough to qualify as a scenic tour area. I pushed my way impatiently past a group of pre-teens taking the cheapie state tour.

Their guide droned on about how *they* might one day earn housing benefits like these if their social outputs were high enough. The spiel was trite, but the kids seemed impressed. They stared up in amazement, for this was a 16 zone; not a single edifice on the block exceeded sixteen stories, and the kids had probably never seen such small buildings before. There were even two twelves on the corner, and I made a note to report that. It's inefficient to waste properly zoned space.

I walked into the stairwell of the corner building and began climbing. Every time I make a call, I promise myself to get into better condition next time. But I never seem to manage it. Even this light smog had me huffing by the time I'd reached the fifth floor, and I was exhausted when I came to the ninth. I paused for breath and then bravely started up again, for the man I was to see lived on the twelfth floor, and the neighborhood wasn't quite nice enough to rate space for such luxuries as elevators.

I noticed that the attractive formica floors had given way to pressed sawdust after the tenth level. Even in nice areas, the higher you go, the cheaper it gets. Finally I reached the twelfth floor and quickly located the correct apartment.

I paused for a moment in front of the door and carefully checked my make-up as I pushed the buzzer. Meeting people on my job always makes me feel curiously inadequate, so I take care to check out my appearance beforehand—especially when I'm wearing a new face, as I was this time. The auburn hair, blue eyes and straight nose looked strange, but there was no denying that they were nicer than what I'd been wearing recently.

I was just slipping the mirror into my thigh-high hose clip when the old man opened the door. He stared at me with questioning, rheumy eyes, then exclaimed, "Harriet! This is impos . . ."

"No," I hurriedly interrupted him. "I'm not Harriet. You must be thinking of someone else."

He shook his head, crestfallen. "Of course you're not. Harriet's dead. Forgive me. But who are you?"

"I'm from the government. A census taker." It's my official title, of course, but I still damn myself for supplying the euphemism every time I use it. "May I come in? I've got some questions that must be answered and some forms for you to fill out." I smiled and stepped forward with apparent confidence.

"The government, oh yes, of course." He moved back and pulled the door wide, so that I wouldn't snag my tunic on the doorjamb.

I looked around the apartment. The feminine influence was striking. Large open areas set off by the color scheme, the precise arrangement of the shelves, the hang of the drapes . . . it was a woman's room, a strong-willed yet sensitive woman. The room seemed to be holding its breath in constant anticipation. It wasn't until the second glance that I noticed that it had been a long time since that woman had been here. It was a refuge out of time, preserved but not expanded upon.

I looked back at the old man, and my eye was caught by a small ring that encircled the middle finger of his left hand. It must have been almost as old as he, for the gold was quite scratched and worn. It was in the shape of a serpent eating its tail; a fine piece of workmanship, and my gaze lingered on it for a moment, admiring the delicately etched scales and lusterless jade eyes of the snake.

I shifted my briefcase from right to left hand and walked toward the couch. "If I may sit down over here, we can get on with my business." I rather liked this new me, both personality and face. I found myself wistfully wishing that the plasto-sculptors would let me keep it. It possessed a certain charm and elegance that was remarkably effective. It seemed to exude self-confidence and its attendant beauty.

"Perhaps," the old man said hesitantly, "you would prefer to wait for my daughter to get home. She's living with me at present, and she usually handles matters like this."

"I'm sure you can help me. It's only a few simple questions."

He seemed hardly to have heard me. "I can't get over how much you look like Harriet. She was my wife, you know."

I did know, but I kept silent. I also didn't mention that

I had been purposely bio-sculpted to resemble her, to put him more at ease. Instead, I said in my best business-like voice, "If we could get down to business, Mr. Rogers?"

"Certainly, Ms . . ." I gave him my name, but he shook his head. "Do you mind if I call you 'Harriet'? You do look so much like her."

I was a trifle annoyed. I didn't particularly want him identifying with me, considering what I was there to do. But our orders are to make it easy, so I simply shrugged and said, "If you wish." I pulled out a pin and some punch tape, hoping that I could finish quickly and get out of there. It was a lonely apartment, permeated with ancient memories.

"Harriet," the old man mused, holding the name on his tongue to savor its sweetness. "She was so wonderful. She used to . . . ." He started guiltily and apologized, "I don't want to bore you."

Call it vicarious living, if you like, but it's the only kind I seem to be able to have any more, so once again I gave in to emotionalism. I decided to hear out his piteous reminiscences. For piteous I was sure they would be. I smiled, no longer disingenuous, for I felt a queer kinship with this antique remnant of lost and lonely humanity. "Please go on. Since you've made me, in a way, her namesake, I'd like to know what sort of a woman she was."

"There's really not much to tell," he sighed, "now that she's gone. She was as beautiful inside as she was outside. I've tried to keep the apartment just the way it was when she died, as a kind of remembrance. My daughter hates it—says we should modernize it, bring it into the twenty-second century. But I couldn't destroy all I have left of Harriet."

"This room can't be all that you have," I insisted. "There must be memories."

A far away look appeared in his eyes. "Indeed there are."

"Then tell me about them."

And he did. From the depths of his withered soul came

the words that were close to song as he recalled his lost and lovely Harriet. Images swirled on images, and light upon shadow, as his mind wandered the happy roads of nostalgia, entrancing me with a hypnotic beauty. Caught by surprise, I entered a world I hadn't known existed. I swam the deceptively deep currents of his mind, and Ariel sang of full fathom five in the back of my mind as I heard his tale of lost love and loneliness. I had thought myself completely beyond such pity, but I was wrong, for now I listened and I shared the warmth of a humanity that had not been mine for longer than I cared to remember.

An hour passed, or was it two? He smiled. "You are a lot like her. I mean, more than just physically. She, too, was a person I could just talk to. She'd always listen and comfort me with silent kindness. Yes, you and she are a lot alike."

I reddened and bowed my head, so he wouldn't see my shame in the comparison.

"Why," he laughed eagerly at the discovery, "you even blush like she did." An excited smile came to his face, as he suddenly thought of something. "Here." He took the magnificent serpent ring from his finger and proffered it. "I'd like you to have this. It's solid gold and the stones are real jade. It's worth quite a bit of money now. I have no one else to give it to."

I shook my head vigorously. "What about your daughter?" I suggested.

"We don't get along too well any more," the old man said sadly. "She's almost forty and still not married. She's got a fiance, but she obviously can't move into his bachelor dorms, and there just don't seem to be any apartments available these days. She's tried to get me to move to one of those old folks' communities, but I couldn't leave here. Harriet and I spent more than half our lives together here."

Again he pushed the ring at me. "I can't take it," I said, my voice wavering. "We're not allowed. . . ."

"Please take it . . . Harriet."

His eyes pleaded, and I couldn't say no. I let him slip the ring on my finger without a word. It was too loose, but it didn't seem to matter.

"Good," he said. "You know, I gave that ring to Harriet when we first got engaged."

So help me, there was an actual tear in my eye. Me, the cold business-woman, the picture of efficiency. Straining to change the subject, I blurted, "Your daughter wasn't always so argumentative, was she?"

"Oh, no. She used to be the most darling little girl the world has ever known. I remember once, when she was about five or six, she was going to the birthday party of a little boy who lived across the courtyard. Halfway there, she tripped in a puddle and got mud all over her party tunic. She knew she shouldn't go in a dirty tunic, so she took it off. There she stood, for all the world to see, naked in the middle of the courtyard." The old man paused, and a sharp crack of laughter burst from his skinny chest. I laughed along with him.

NOW!

"You even laugh like she did," he was saying. Instead of answering I activated the battery I had and, leaning forward, tenderly pushed the hair away from his forehead.

He stiffened and fell forward onto the coffee table, dead. But a smile was engraved forever on his ancient features.

I left then, carefully closing the door behind me. The apartment belonged to someone else now, and they wouldn't want their property disturbed.

The snack shop was dim. I suspect that's why my client had asked me to report there. Somehow, people seem to think that darkness assuages guilt.

I looked around, peering over the heads of the citizens scheduled for free time on this shift. Because of the nature of my job I can't be properly scheduled and, looking around at these happy, regulated people, I regretted it. I blinked as my eyes became accustomed to the light, and I saw the client. She had managed to snag two seats in the corner. She didn't look very prepossessing: thin, weedy, dressed in a severe tunic that accentuated her fortyish figure. I wondered how she had managed to rout the competition for that extra seat. On the table, there were several empty glasses. That fit the pattern I'd expected, and I nodded to myself. Alcohol, too, assuages guilt. I know.

I walked briskly over and stood beside her without saying a word. It took a moment for her to look up at me. When she did, I could see that her eyes were glazed over, but whether from alcohol or tears, I couldn't tell.

She didn't recognize me for a second. When she did, she blurtingly invited me to take the empty seat. Silently, I did.

For years, it seemed, we sat there, staring at one another across the table. She obviously wanted me to speak first. I refused to give her the satisfaction. Finally, she broke the silence. "It's over, isn't it?"

"He's dead, if that's what you mean." I enjoyed the shocked expression on her face. "The body will be disposed of before your return. The apartment is vacated." I've found it easier on myself if I'm blunt.

She looked down at her lap. "You needn't put it that way," she complained, wringing her hands frantically. "It makes it sound so . . . so inhuman."

"It's what you wanted, isn't it?"

"No!" she almost shrieked. Her voice rose on a sudden note of near hysteria, and she was oblivious to the people who turned their heads to look. "I didn't want it that way. But he wouldn't leave that mausoleum. Don't you see, this is my last chance to get a husband. I need that apartment. There's no room anywhere these days. Why wouldn't he move to the retirement village? I didn't want to have him killed."

I just stared at her.

She became quieter. "And . . . and then there's the

population explosion . . . you know, the old should make room for the younger people. It's their duty, they've already lived their lives. It's not fair. I'm entitled to my chance."

I'd read our ads, too. They were designed for people like her. "May I see your credit card, please?"

"What? Oh . . . oh yes." She fumbled through her stocking pocket and fished out her Universal Credit Card. While she was working on another drink, I calmly jotted down the price, including tax, on a sales slip. "Would you like to check my addition?" I asked.

"I'm sure it's all right." She was beginning to resume what must be her normal stuffy manner. "It *was* painless, wasn't it?"

"Absolutely," I said without looking up. I didn't want to see the greedy expression in her eyes that I could hear in her voice, so I concentrated on copying her serial number onto the slip. "At the proper moment, I activated a device that destroyed his brain tissue. His sensory apparatus was the first to go—shorted out the nerves. He couldn't feel a thing. I'll need your signature on the bottom here." I handed her the charge slip.

She scribbled "Lisa Rogers" hurriedly along the line and handed it back. "This is deductible, isn't it?"

I wanted to spit at her. Instead, I said, "Yes, Miss Rogers, government-administered euthanasia is completely tax deductible." I returned her card, along with a carbon of the sales slip. "You can use this as a receipt."

Downing what was left of her drink in one quick gulp, she got up from the table. "Thanks. Now, if you'll excuse me, I have an appointment with my fiance at the registrar's office." I nodded an "of course."

She practically ran out of the restaurant.

I sat back in my chair and ordered a drink of my own. Just one. That's all I allow myself now. Another woman, who might as well have been Lisa Rogers' double, immediately rushed over and grabbed the empty chair.

I took off the old man's ring and looked at it. In the dim

restaurant, it was difficult to see how battered it really was. The gold reflected the feeble light like a shiny yellow mirror and the jade almost glowed with a milky-green luminescence.

My drink came, and I put the ring down on the table. It looked even more like a hideous serpent eating its own tail. As I sipped slowly, I could feel the ring watching me with a fixed, unblinking stare. I stared back at it. For some reason, the design reminded me of the client who'd just left.

My drink seemed to be lacking its customary lift, so I dropped the plastic tumbler, still half-full, into the disposal unit set in the center of the table.

As I stood up, I found a stinging in my eyes, though the inside of the snack shop wasn't particularly smoggy. I blinked, trying to stop the smarting, as I dropped the old man's ring into the maw of the disposal unit, inserted my nose-plugs, and walked out into the sulphur-yellow sunlight.

Mutation Planet

BARRINGTON J. BAYLEY

THE VAST and brooding landscape, filled with ominous mutterings, ground-trembling rumblings, stretched all around in an infinity of gloom. The mountainous form of *Dominus* moved across this landscape at speed, like a massy shadow, heavy with power and sullenly majestic. Above him the opaque sky, lurid and oppressively close, flared intermittently and discharged sheets of lightning that were engulfed in the distant hills. In the instant before some creature fed on the electric glare, the dimness would be relieved, outlining endless, uneven expanses of near-barren soil. *Dominus*, however, took no sensory advantage of these flashes; his inputs covered a wider, more reliable range of impressions.

As he sped through his domain he scattered genetic materials to either side of him. These would dampen down evolutionary activity for miles around and ensure that no lifeform would arise that could inconvenience him or interfere with the roadway over which he moved. Built by himself as one of the main instruments of his control over his environment, this roadway spanned the whole eight thousand miles of the planet's single continent, and was a uniform quarter of a mile wide; side roads diverged, at irregular intervals, into the larger peninsulas. Since the substance of the roadbed was quasi-organic, having been extruded by organs he possessed for that purpose, *Dominus* could, moreover, sense instantly any attack, damage, or unacceptable occurrence taking place on any part of it.

After leaving the interminable plain the road undulated over a series of hills, clinging always to the profile of the land, and swept down into a gigantic bowl-like valley. Here the gloom took on the darkness of a pit, but lifeforms were more copious. By the light of the flickering lightning flashes, or by that of the more diffuse radiations employed by *Dominus*, they could be seen skulking out there in the valley, a scattering of unique shapes. They were absolutely motionless, since none dared to move while *Dominus* passed by. Leagues further afield lights winked and radio pulses beamed out as the more powerful entities living up the slopes of the valley signalled their submission.

Dominus dosed the valley heavily with genetic mist, then surged up the opposite wall. As he swept over onto a table-land a highly-charged lightning bolt came sizzling down, very close; he caught it in one of his conductors and stored the charge in his accumulators. It was then, while he raced away from the valley, that his radar sense spotted the unidentifiable object descending through the cloud blanket. Puzzled, *Dominus* slowed down to scarcely a hundred miles per hour. This was the first unusual event for several millennia. He could not, at first, account for it.

The strangeness lay in the fact that the object was so large: not very much smaller than *Dominus* himself. (Its shape, though new to him, was of no account—even at the low, controlled level of mutation thousands of different lifeforms continued to evolve.) Also, it was moving through the air without the visible benefit of wings of any kind. Come to that, a creature of such bulk could not be lifted by wings at all.

Where had it evolved? In the sky? Most unlikely. The plethora of flying forms that had once spent their lives winging through the black, static-drenched cloud layer had almost—thanks to *Dominus*—died out. Over the ages his mutation-damping mist, rising on the winds, had accumulated there, and without a steady mutation rate the flying forms had been unable to survive the ravages of their environment and each other.

Then from where? Some part of the continent receiving only scant surveillance from *Dominus*? He was inclined to doubt this also. The entity he observed could not have developed without many generations of mutation, which would have come to his notice before now.

Neither was the ocean any more likely a source. True, *Dominus* carried out no surveillance there. But a great deal of genetic experience was required to survive on the land surface. Emergent amphibia lacked that experience and were unable to gain a foothold. For that reason oceanic evolution seemed to have resigned itself to a purely submarine existence.

One other possibility remained: the emptiness beyond the atmospheric covering. For *Dominus* this possibility was theoretical only, carrying no emotional ambience. Up to now *this* world had absorbed his psychic energies: *this* was life and existence.

Due to this ambiguity *Dominus* did not act immediately but kept in check the strong instinctive urges that were triggered off. Interrupting his pan-continental patrol for the first time in millennia, he followed the object to its landing place. Then he settled down patiently to await developments.

Eliot Harst knew exactly where to find Balbain. He climbed the curving ramp to the upper part of the dome-shaped spaceship and opened a door. The alien was standing at the big observation window, looking out on to Five's (whatever system they were in, they always named the planets in order from their primary) blustering semi-night.

The clouds glowed patchily as though bombs were being let off among them; the lightning boomed and crashed. The tall, thin alien ignored all this, however. His attention was fixed on the gigantic organism they had already named *Dominus*, which was slumped scarcely more than a mile away. Eliot had known him to gaze at it, unmoving, for hours.

"The experiment has worked out after all," he said. "Do you want to take a look?"

Balbain tore his gaze from the window and looked at Eliot. He came from a star which, to Eliot, was only a number in Solsystem's catalogs. His face was partly obscured by the light breathing mask he wore to supplement ship atmosphere. (The aliens all seemed to think that human beings were more sensitive to discomfort than themselves: everything on the ship was biased towards the convenience of Eliot and his assistant Alanie.) But over the mask Balbain's bright bird-like eyes were visible, darting from his bony, fragile and quite unhuman skull.

"The result is positive?" he intoned in an oddly hollow, resonant voice.

"It would seem so."

"It is as we already knew. I do not wish to see the offspring at present, but thank you for informing me."

With that he returned to the window and seemed to become abruptly unaware of Eliot's presence.

Sighing, the Earthman left the chamber. A few yards further along the gallery he stopped at a second door. Jingling a bell to announce his presence, he entered a small bare cell and gave the same message as before to its occupant.

Abrak came from a star as far from Balbain's as the latter was from Solsystem. When fully erect he stood less than five feet in height and had a skin like corded cloth: full of neat folds and wavy grains. At the moment he squatted on the naked floor, his skeletal legs folded under him in an extraordinary double-jointed way that Eliot found quite grotesque.

Abrak's voice was crooning and smooth, and contained unnerving infra-sound beats that made a human listener feel uneasy and slightly dizzy—Eliot already knew, in fact, that Abrak could, if he wished, kill him merely by speaking: by voicing quiet vibrations of just the right frequency to cripple his internal organs.

"So the picture we have built is vindicated?" he replied to Eliot's announcement, pointing a masked, dog-like face towards the Earthman.

"There can be little doubt of it."

"I will view the offspring." The alien rose in one swift motion.

Eliot had already decided that there was no point in reporting to the fifth member of the team: Zeed, the third of the non-humans. He appeared to take no more interest in their researches.

He led the way back down the connecting ramps, through the interior of the spaceship which he had been finding increasingly depressing of late. More and more it reminded him of a hurriedly-built air-raid shelter, devoid of decoration, rough-hewn, dreary and echoing.

Balbain's people had built the ship. Eliot could recall his excitement on learning of its purpose, an excitement that doubled when it transpired he had a chance of joining it. For the ship was travelling from star to star on a quest for knowledge. And as it journeyed it occasionally recruited another scientist from a civilization sufficiently advanced, if he would make a useful member of the team. So far, in addition to the original Balbain, there had been Zeed, Abrak (none of these being their real, unpronounceable names, but convenience names for human benefit: transliterations or syllabic equivalents), and, of course, Elliot and Alanie.

Alanie had been, for Eliot, one of the fringe benefits —another being that when they returned to Solsystem they would take back with them a prodigious mass of data, a countless number of discoveries, and would become immortally famous. The aliens, recognizing that human sexuality is more than usually needful, had offered to allow a male-female pair as Solsystem's contribution. Eliot had discovered that his prospect of a noble ordeal was considerably mitigated by the thought of spending that time alone with his selected team-mate: Alanie Leitner, vivacious, companionable, with an I.Q. of 190 (slightly better than Eliot's own, in fact) and an experienced all-round researcher. The perfect assistant for him, the selection board had assured him, and he had found little in their verdict to disagree with, then or since.

But the real thrill had been in the thing itself: in being part of a voyage of discovery that transcended racial barriers, in the uplifting demonstration that wherever intelligence arose it formed the same aspiration: to know, to examine, to reveal the universe.

Mind was mind: a universal constant.

Unfortunately he and Alanie seemed to be drifting apart from their alien travelling companions, to understand them less and less. The truth was that he and Alanie were doing all the work. They would arrive at a system and begin a survey; yet very quickly the interest of the others would die off and the humans would be left to carry out all the real research, draw the conclusions and write up the reports completely unaided. As a matter of fact Zeed now took scarcely any interest at all and did not stir from his quarters for months on end.

Eliot found it quite inexplicable, especially since Balbain and Abrak, both of whom impressed one by the strength of their intellects, admitted that since leaving Solsystem much had been discovered that was novel.

At the bottom of the ramp he led Abrak into the laboratory section. And there to greet them was Alanie Leitner: a wide, slightly sulky mouth in a pale face; a strong nose, steady brown eyes and auburn, nearly reddish hair cut squarely on the nape of the neck. And even in her white laboratory smock the qualities of her figure were evident.

Though constructed of the same concrete-like stuff as the rest of the spaceship, the laboratory was made more cheerful by being a place of work. At the far end was the test chamber. Abrak made his way there and peered through the thick window. The parent specimen they had begun with lay up against the wall of the circular chamber, apparently dying after its birth-giving exertions. It was about the size of a dog, but spider-like, with the addition of a rearward clump of tissue that sprouted an untidy bunch of antenna-type sensors.

Its offspring, lying inert a few yards away, offered absolutely no resemblance to the spider-beast. A dense-looking, slipper-shaped object, somewhat smaller than the parent, it could have been no more than a lump of wood or metal.

"It's too soon yet to be able to say what it can do," Alanie said, joining them at the window.

Abrak was silent for a while. "Is it not possible that this is a larval, immature stage, thus accounting for the absence of likeness?" he suggested then.

"It's conceivable, certainly," Eliot answered. "But we think the possibility is remote. For one thing we are pretty certain that the offspring was already adult and fully grown, or practically so, when it was born. For another, the fact that the parent reproduced at all is pretty convincing confirmation of our theory. Added to everything else we know, I don't feel disposed towards accepting any other explanation."

"Agreed," Abrak replied. "Then we must finally accept that the Basic Polarity does not obtain here on Five."

"That's right."

Although he should have become accustomed to the

idea by now Eliot's brain still went spinning when he thought of it and all it entailed.

Scientifically speaking the notion of the Basic Polarity went back, as far as Solsystem was concerned, to the Central Dogma. In a negative sense, it also went back to the related Koestler's Question, posed late in the 20th Century.

The Central Dogma expressed the keystone of genetics: that the interaction between *gene* and *soma* was a one-way traffic. The genes formed the body. But nothing belonging to the body, or anything that it experienced, could modify the genes or have any effect on the next generation. Thus there was no inheritance of acquired characteristics; evolution was conducted over immensely long periods of time through random mutations resulting from cosmic radiation, or through chemical accidents in the gene substance itself.

Why, Koestler asked, should this be so? A creature that could refashion its genes, endowing its offspring with the means to cope with the hazards *it* had experienced, would have a great advantage in the struggle for survival. Going further, a creature that could lift itself by its bootstraps and produce a superior type in this way would have an even greater advantage. Furthermore, Koestler argued that direct reshaping of the genes should be perfectly within the capabilities of organic life, using chemical agents.

So the absence of such a policy in organic life was counter-survival, a curious, glaring neglect on the part of nature. The riddle was answered, by Koestler's own contemporaries, in the following manner: if the *soma*, on the basis of its experiences, was to modify the gene-carrying DNA, then the modification would have to be planned and executed by the instinctive functions of the nervous system, or by whatever corresponded to those functions in any conceivable creature. But neither the instinctive brains of the higher orders, nor the primitive ganglia of the lower orders, had the competence to carry out this work: acting purely by past-conditioned responses, they had no apprehension of the future and would not have been able to relate experience to genetic alteration. Hence life had been dependent on random influences: radiation and accident.

For direct gene alteration to be successful, Koestler's rebuttors maintained, some form of intellect would be needed. Primitive animals did not have this; if the gene-changing animal existed, then that animal was man, and man worked not through innate bodily powers but by artificial manipulation of the chromosomes. Even then, his efforts had been partial and inept: the eradication of defective genes to rectify the increasing incidence of deformity; the creation of a few new animals that had quickly sickened and died.

And with that the whole matter of Koestler's Question had been quietly forgotten. The Central Dogma was reinstated, not merely as an arbitrary fact but as a necessary principle. If Koestler's Question had any outcome, then it was in the recognition of the Basic Polarity: the polarity between individual and species. Because the species, not the individual, had to be the instrument of evolution. If the Central Dogma did not hold, then species would not need to exist at all (and neither, incidentally, would sex). The rate of change would be so swift that there would be nothing to hold them together—and any that did exist, because of some old-fashioned immutability of their genes, would rapidly be wiped out. And indeed the Basic Polarity seemed to be the fundamental form of life everywhere in the universe, as Balbain, Abrak and Zeed all confirmed.

Eliot was thinking of renaming Five "Koestler's Planet."

On a world where all traces of the past could be wiped out overnight, they would probably never know exactly what had happened early in Five's biological evolution to overthrow the Central Dogma. Presumably the instinctive functions had developed, not intelligence exactly, but a unique kind of telegraph between their experience of the external world and the microscopic coding of the germ plasm. It would, as Alanie pointed out, only have to happen once, and that once could even be at the bacterial level. The progeny of a single individual would rapidly supplant all other fauna. In the explosion of organic development that followed it would be but a short step before gene alteration became truly inventive; intellectual abilities would soon arise to serve this need.

It had been some time before the idea had dawned on them that Five might be a planet of single-instance species; in other words, of no species at all. There was one four-eyed stoat; one elephantine terror; one leaping prong; one blanket (their name for a creature of that description which spent most of its time merely lying on the ground). In fact there was a bewildering variety of forms of which only one example could be found. But there were one or two exceptions to the rule—or so they had thought. They had videotaped six specimens of a type of multi-legged snake. Only later had they discovered that the resemblance between them was a case of imitation, of convergent evolution among animals otherwise unrelated.

So they had been forced, reluctantly, to accept the evidence of their eyes, and later, of the electron microscope. But only now, in the last hour, was Eliot one hundred percent convinced of it.

Another thing that had made him cautious was the sheer degree of knowledge and intelligence consistent with this level of biological engineering. He would have expected every creature on the planet to display intelligence at least equivalent to the human. Instead the animals here were just that—animals. Clever, ferocious animals, but content to inhabit their ecological niches and evincing no intellectual temperament.

All, that is, except *Dominus*.

They called him *Dominus* because he had the aspect of being king of all he surveyed. He must have weighed a thousand tons at least. He was also owner of the road system, which at first they had taken to be evidence of a civilization, or at least the remains of one. It was now clear, however, that the road had been *Dominus'* own idea —or, more probably, his parent's idea.

The great beast had demonstrated his understanding when they had gone out and tried to trap specimens for laboratory study. The exercise had proved to be dangerous and nearly impossible. Five's fauna were the universe's greatest experts at not getting killed, caught or trapped, and had responded not merely with claw, fang and evasive speed, but with electricity, poison gas, infra-sound (Abrak's own speciality), corrosives of various types they had still not classified but which had scared them very much, thick strands of unknown substance spun swiftly out from spinnerets and carried on the wind, slugs of pure iron ejected from porcupine-like quills with the velocity of rifle bullets, and—believe it or not—organically generated laser beams.

Retreating after one of their sorties to the shelter of their spaceship's force shield, the hunters had been about to give up and go back inside.

Alanie had said: "Let's get off this planet before one of those things throws a fusion beam at us."

And then *Dominus* had acted. Rushing down, like a smaller hill himself, from the hill where he had parked himself, he had advanced driving several smaller animals before him. Finally they had delivered themselves almost at the scientists' feet and promptly fallen unconscious. *Dominus* had then returned to the hill-top, where he had squatted motionless ever since. And Eliot, blended with his amazement, had felt the same thrill and transcendence that had overwhelmed him at the first arrival of Balbain's starship.

Dominus understood their wants! He was helping them!

Conceivably he could be communicated with. But that problem had to wait. They got the creatures inside and put them under adequate restraint. Then Eliot and Alanie went immediately to work.

The creatures' genes followed the standard pattern produced by matter on planetary surfaces everywhere: coded helices forming a group of chromosomes. The code was doublet and not triplet, as it was on Earth, but that in itself was not unusual: Abrak's genes also were in doublet code. More significantly, the single gonad incorporated a molecular factory, vast by microscopic standards, able to dispatch a chemical operator to any specific gene in a selected germ cell. And, furthermore, a chain of command could be discerned passing into the spinal column (where there was a spinal column) and thence to the brain (where there was a brain).

Eliot had written in his journal:

I get the impression that we are witness to a fairly late stage of Five's evolutionary development. For one thing, life here is relatively sparse, as though fierce competition has thinned down numbers rather than increased them, leading to a more subdued mode of existence. There are no predators; defensive mutations on the part of a potential prey would no doubt make it unprofitable to be a carnivore. The vegetation on Five conforms to the Basic Polarity and so presumably predates the overthrow of the Central Dogma, but it survives patchily in the form of scrub savannahs and a few small forests, and in many areas does not exist at all. The majority of animals own a patch of vegetation which they defend against all comers with an endless array of natural weapons, but they eat only in order to obtain body-building materials—proteins and trace elements—and not to provide energy, which they obtain by soaking up the ubiquitous lightning discharges. Some animals have altogether abandoned any dependence of an external food chain: they carry out the whole of the anabolic process themselves, taking the requisite elements and minerals from soil and air and metabolizing all their requirements using the energy from this same lightning.

It has occurred to us that all the animals here are potentially immortal. Ageing is a species-characteristic, the life-span being adjusted to the maximum benefit of the species, not of the individual. If all our conclusions are correct, an organism on Five would continue to live a self-contained life until meeting some pressing exigency it was not able to master; only then would it reproduce to create a more talented version of itself and afterwards, perhaps, permit itself to die. This notion suggests that a test may be possible.

The slipper organism was the outcome of that test. They had placed the spider-thing in a chamber and subjected it to stress. They had bombarded it with pressure, heat, missiles, and various other discomforts suggested by the details of its metabolism. And they had waited to see whether it would react by "conceiving" and ultimately giving birth to another creature better than itself.

Of course, the new organism would be designed to accomplish one thing above all: escape. Eliot was curious now to see how the slipper would attempt it.

"Might it not be dangerous?" Abrak questioned mildly. Eliot flipped a switch. A thick slab of dull metal slid down to occlude the window. Instead, they could continue to watch through a vidcamera.

"I'd like to see it get through that," he boasted. "Carbon and titanium alloy a foot thick. It's surrounded by it."

"You are being unsubtle," said Abrak. "Perhaps the beast will rely on trickery."

Alanie gave a deep sigh that strained her full breasts voluptuously against the fabric of her smock. "Well, what now?" she asked. "We've been here six months. I think we've solved the basic mystery of the place. Isn't it time we were moving on?"

"I'd like to stay longer," Eliot said thoughtfully. "I want to see if we can get into communication with *Dominus*."

"But how?" she asked, sitting down at a bench and waving her hand. "Communication is a species-characteristic. He probably would never understand what language is."

"And yet already he's given us help, so we *can* communicate after a fashion," Eliot argued.

A warning sound came from Abrak. Something was happening on the screen looking into the test chamber.

The slipper organism had decided to act. Gliding smoothly to the far side of the chamber, nearest the skin of the ship, it pressed its tapered end against the wall. Abruptly the toe of the slipper ignited into an intense glare too bright for the vidcamera to handle. An instant later fumes billowed up and filled the chamber, obscuring everything.

By the time they cleared sufficiently for the onlookers to see anything, the slipper had made its exit through the wall of the chamber, and thence through the ship's skin, by burning a channel whose edges were still white-hot.

"I think," said Eliot somberly, "it might just have been a fusion beam, or something just as good."

He paused uncertainly. Then he flung open a cupboard and began pulling out gear. "Come on," he said, "We're going after our specimen."

"But it will kill us," Alanie protested.

"Not if *Dominus* helps us again. And somehow I think he will."

Dominus is an intelligent being, he told himself. Intelligent beings are motivated by curiosity and a sense of co-operation with other intelligent beings. His hunt for the slipper was, in fact, impelled more by the desire to prompt *Dominus* into co-operating with them again than by any interest in regaining the slipper itself, which could well be far away by now.

"But, once having recaptured the creature, how will you retain it?" inquired Abrak, looking meaningfully at the gaping hole in the chamber.

"We'll keep it under sedation," Eliot said, buckling on a protective suit.

Minutes later he stood at the foot of the spaceship. Besides the protective suit he was armed with a gun that fired recently prepared sleep darts (they had worked on the slipper's parent, following a biochemical analysis of that creature) and a cylinder that extruded a titanium mesh net.

Though evincing less enthusiasm, Alanie and Abrak had nevertheless followed him, despite his waiver to the girl. Abrak was unprotected, carried no weapons, and relied on his flimsy ship mask to take care of Five's atmosphere.

The environment boomed, flickered and flashed all around them. To Eliot's surprise the slipper could be seen less than a hundred yards away, lying quietly in the beams of their torches.

He glanced up towards the bulk of *Dominus*, then stepped resolutely forward, aware of the footsteps of the others behind him.

Up on the hill, *Dominus* began to move. Eliot stopped and stared up at him exultantly.

"Eliot," Abrak crooned at his elbow, "I strongly recommend caution. Specifically, I recommend a return to the ship."

Eliot made no answer. His mind was racing, wondering what gesture he could make to *Dominus* when the vast beast recaptured the slipper and returned it to them.

He was quite, quite wrong.

Dominus halted some distance away, and extruded a tongue, or tentacle, travelling at ground level almost too fast for the eye to follow. In little more than a second or two it had flashed across the sandy soil and scrubby grass, seized on Alanie, lifted her bodily from the ground and whisked her away before a scream could form in her throat. Eliot noticed, blurrily, that the entire length of the tentacle was covered with wriggling wormy protuberances.

Even as Alanie was withdrawn into the body of *Dominus* Eliot was running forward, howling wildly and firing his dart gun. Light footsteps pattered to his rear; surprisingly strong, bony arms restrained his. "It is no use, Eliot. *Dominus* has taken her. He is not what you thought."

Early on *Dominus* had perceived that the massy object, which he now accepted came from beyond the atmosphere, was not itself a lifeform but a lifeform's construct. The idea was already a familiar one: artifacts were rare on his planet—biological evolution was simpler—but there had been a brief period when they had proliferated, attaining increasing orders of sophistication until they had nearly devastated the continent. Stored in his redundant genes *Dominus* still retained all the knowledge of his ancestors on that score.

From the construct emerged undoubtedly organic entities, and it was in this that the mystery lay: there were several of them. *Dominus* spent some time mulling over this inexplicable fact. Who, then, was owner of the construct? He noted that, within limits, all the foreign lifeforms bore a resemblance to one another, and reminded himself that ecological convergence was an occasional phenomenon within his own domain. Could this convergence have been carried further and some kind of *ecological common action* (he formed the concept with difficulty) have arisen among entities occupying the same ecological niche? He reasoned that he should entertain no preconceptions as to the courses evolution might take under unimaginably alien conditions. Some relationship even more incomprehensible to him might be the case.

So he had been patient, watching jealously as the lifeforms surveyed part of his domain in a flying artifact, but doing nothing. Then they had attempted, but failed, to capture some native organisms. Wanting to see what would take place, *Dominus* had delivered a few to them.

When he saw the mutated lifeform emerge from the construct on its escape bid, he knew it was as he had anticipated. The aliens must have made a genetic analysis of all their specimens. The massy construct was sealed against *Dominus'* mutation-damping genes, and within that isolation they had carried out an experiment, subjecting one of the specimens to a challenge situation and prompting it to reproduce.

Dominus could forbear no longer. He issued the slipper with a stern command to stay fast. It was sufficiently its father's son to know what the consequences of disobeying him would be. Three alien lifeforms emerged in pursuit. To begin with, *Dominus* took one of the pair that were so nearly identical.

Alanie Leitner floated, deep within *Dominus'* body, in a sort of protein jelly. Mercifully, she was quite dead. Thousands of nerve-thin tendrils entered her body to carry out a brief but adequate somatic exploration. At the same time billions upon billions of RNA operators migrated to her gonads (there were two of them) and sifted down to the genetic level where they analyzed her chromosomes with perfect completeness.

"It killed her," Eliot was repeating in a stunned, muttering voice. "It killed her."

Abrak had persuaded him to return to the ship. They found that Balbain had abandoned his vigil and was pacing the central chamber situated over the laboratory. His bird-eyes glittered at them with unusual fervor.

"We can delay no further," he boomed. "*Dominus'* qualities cannot be gainsaid. The sense of him is overpowering. Therefore my quest is at an end. I shall return home."

"No!" crooned Abrak suddenly, in a hard tone Eliot had not heard him use before. "This planet also holds the promise of answering *our* requirements."

"You take second place. *I* originated this expedition, and therefore you are pre-empted."

"We shall see who will pre-empt whom," Abrak barked.

While the import of the exchange was lost on Eliot, he was bewildered at seeing these two, whom he had thought of as dispassionate men (beings, anyway) of science, quarreling and snarling like wild dogs. So palpable was the ferocity that he was startled out of his numbness and waved his arms placatingly as though to separate them.

"Gentlemen! Is this any way for a scientific expedition to conduct itself?"

The aliens glanced at him. Balbain's mask had become wet—perhaps with the exudations of some emotion—and partly transparent. Through it Eliot saw the gaping, square mouth that never closed.

"Let us laugh," Balbain said, addressing Abrak.

They both gave vent to regular chugging expulsions of air; it was a creaking monotone, devoid of mirth but a weird simulation of human laughter. Neither species, to Eliot's knowledge, were endowed with a sense of humor at all; once or twice before he had heard them use this travesty to indicate, in human speech, where they believed laughter would be appropriate.

He felt chilled. A feeling of *alienness* wafted towards him from the two beings, whom previously he had regarded as companions.

Balbain made a vague gesture. "We know that you judge us by your own standards," he said, "but it is not so. Like you, we each came on this expedition to satisfy cravings inherent in our species. But those cravings are different from yours and from each other. . . ."

His voice softened and became almost caressing. Bending his head slightly, he indicated the wall of the ship, as though to direct Eliot's attention outside.

"Try to imagine what evolution means here on Five. It takes not eons or millions of years to produce a biological invention, but only a few months. The Basic Polarity is not here to soften life's blows; competition is so intense that Five is the toughest testing ground in the universe. The result of all this should be obvious. What we have here is the most capable, potentially the most powerful source of life that could possibly exist. And *Dominus* is the fulfillment of that process. The most intolerant, the most *domineering*—" he put special emphasis on the word—"entity that the universe can produce!"

"Domineering?" echoed Eliot, frowning.

"But of course! Think for a moment: what special

quality must a creature develop on Five in order to make itself safe? The ability to dominate everything around it! *Dominus* has that quality to the ultimate degree. He is the Lord, in submission to whom my species can at last find peace of mind."

Balbain spoke with such passion and in such a strange manner that Eliot could only stand and stare. Abrak spoke softly, turning his fox's snout towards him.

"It is hard for Balbain to convey what he is feeling," he crooned. "Perhaps I can explain it to your intellect, at least. First, the romantic picture you harbor concerning the fellowship of sentient minds is, I am afraid, quite incorrect. Mentalities are even more diverse in character than are physical forms. What goads us into action is not what goads you."

"Then we cannot understand one another?" Eliot said.

"Only indirectly. In almost every advanced species there is a central drive that comes from its evolutionary history and overrides all other emotions—in its best specimens. This overriding urge gives the race as a whole its existential meaning. To other races it might look futile or even ridiculous—as, indeed, yours does to us—but to the species concerned it is a universal imperative, self-evident and inescapable."

He paused to allow Eliot to absorb what he was saying. While Balbain looked on, seeming scarcely any less agitated, he continued calmly: "For reasons too complex to describe, life on Balbain's world developed a submission-orientation. The physical conditions there, much harsher than what you are accustomed to, caused living beings to enter into an elaborate network of relationships in which each sought, not to dominate, but to *be* dominated by some other power, the stronger the better. This craving is thus the compass needle that guides Balbain's species. To them it is self-fulfilment, the inner meaning of the universe itself."

Eliot glanced at Balbain. The revelation made him feel uncomfortable.

"But how *can* it be?"

"Every species sees its own fixation as expressing the hidden nature of the universe. Do not you?"

Eliot brushed aside the question, which he did not understand. "But what's all this about *Dominus?*"

"Why, he represents the other half of this craving. His is a mentality of compulsive domination. He rules this planet, and would rule any planet with which he came in contact. Balbain knows this. With *Dominus* to command them, his people will feel something of completeness."

A small flash of insight came to Eliot. "That is *his* reason for this expedition?"

"Correct. On his own world Balbain is a sort of knight, or saint, who has set out in search of this . . . Holy Grail."

"We shall offer ourselves as *Dominus'* slaves," Balbain boomed hollowly. "It is his nature to assume the position of master."

Eliot tried to fight off his feeling of revulsion, but failed. "You're . . . insane . . ." he whispered.

Once again Abrak's fake laughter chugged out. "But Balbain's assessment of *Dominus* is perfectly correct. Five *is* the source of potentially the greatest, and in many ways the strangest, power that existence is capable of producing, and *Dominus*, at this moment in time, is the highest expression of that power. There can be others— and that is why it is of interest to my people! We also have an existential craving!"

His snout turned menacingly towards Balbain. Eliot thought suddenly of his frightening ability to generate infra-sound.

"You will have no opportunity to satisfy it. Nothing will prevent us from becoming the property of *Dominus.*" Balbain's words throbbed with passion. He was like an animal in heat.

The two began to circle one another warily. Eliot backed towards the door, afraid of infra-sound. He saw Abrak's snout open behind his mask.

Shuddering waves of vibration passed through his body.

But, incredibly, in the same second Abrak died. His body was converting, from the head down, into sand-colored dust which streamed across the chamber in a rustling spray.

Balbain's claw-like hand held the presumed source of this phenomenon: a device consisting of a cluster of tubes. When nothing remained of Abrak he put it away in a fold of his garment.

"Fear not," he said to Eliot in a conciliatory tone. "You have no reason to obstruct me. After I take home the glad tidings, you can return to Solsystem."

Eliot did not answer, but merely stood as if paralyzed. Balbain gave a brief, apologetic burst of hollow, fake laughter, seeming to guess what was on Eliot's mind.

"As for Abrak, reserve your judgment on my action. I have given him what he desired—though to tell the truth he would have preferred the fate of your female, Alanie."

"Alanie," Eliot repeated. "How can we be sure she's dead? It may be keeping her alive. I don't know why you murdered Abrak, Balbain, but if you want me to help you, then help me to get Alanie back. Then I'll do anything you ask of me."

"Defy *Dominus*?" Balbain looked at him pityingly. "Pointless, hopeless, perverted dreams. . . ."

Suddenly he rushed past Eliot and through the door. Eliot heard his feet clattering on the downward ramp.

The Earthman sat down and buried his face in his hands.

A minute or two later he felt impelled to turn on the external view screen to get another look at *Dominus*. A bizarre sight met his eyes. Balbain, about halfway between *Dominus* and the ship, had prostrated himself before the great beast and was making small gestures whose meanings were known only to himself. Eliot switched off the screen. A few minutes later, not having heard Balbain return, he looked again. There was no sign of the alien.

He was not sure how long he then sat there, trying to decide what best next to do, before a noise made him look up. The interstellar expedition's only other surviving member was entering the chamber.

Zeed was the least humanoid of all the team. He walked on limbs that could be said to constitute a pair of legs, except that they could also reconstitute themselves into tentacles, or a bunch of sticks, or a number of other devices to accommodate him to locomotion over a variety of different surfaces. Above these limbs a short dumpy body of indeterminate shape was hidden by a thick cloak which also hid his arms. Above this, a head of sorts: speckled golden eyes that did not at first look like eyes, other organs buried within fluted, bony grooves arranged in a symmetrical pattern.

The voice in which he spoke to Eliot, however, could have passed as human, although no mouth appeared to move.

"Explanations are superfluous," he said, moving into the chamber and looking down on Eliot. "I have consulted the ship's log."

Eliot nodded. The log, of course, automatically recorded everything that took place within the ship.

"It appears that Balbain could not constrain himself and has forfeited his life," Zeed continued. "It is not surprising. However, it determines our end, also, since only Abrak and Balbain knew how to pilot the ship."

This was news to Eliot, but in his present state the prospect of death caused him little alarm.

"Did *you* know Balbain's secret reason for this mission?" he asked.

"Of course. But it was no secret. Your people, being ignorant of alien races, made a presumption concerning its nature." Gliding smoothly on his versatile legs, Zeed moved to the view screen and made a full circle scan of their surroundings. Then he turned back to Eliot. "Perhaps it is a disappointment to you."

"Why did Balbain want any of us along at all?" Eliot said wearily. "Just to make use of us?"

"In a way. But we were all making use of each other.

The universe is vast and quite mysterious, Eliot. It is an unfathomable darkness in which creatures arise having no common ground with each other. Hence, if they meet they may not be able to comprehend one another. Here in this ship we act as antennae for one another. We are not so alien to one another that we cannot communicate, yet sufficiently unalike so that each may understand some phenomena we encounter that the others cannot."

"So that's what we are," Eliot said resentfully. "A star-travelling menagerie."

"An ark, in which each has a separate quest. Yours is the obsession to acquire knowledge. We do not share it, but the data you are collecting is your reward for the services you may, at some time, have been able to render one of us. You were enjoying yourselves too much for us to disillusion you concerning ourselves."

"But how can you *not* share it?" Eliot exclaimed. "Scientific inquiry is fundamental to intelligence, surely? How else can one ever understand the universe?"

"But others do not want to understand it, Eliot. That is only your own relationship to it; your chief ethological feature, whether you recognize it or not. You would still have joined this expedition, for instance, if it had meant giving up sex for the rest of your life."

"And yet you have a scientific culture and travel in spaceships."

"A matter of mere practicality. Pure, abstract science exists only for *homo sapiens*—I have not encountered it elsewhere. Other races carry out investigations only for the material benefits they bring. As an extreme example, think of *Dominus*: he, and probably countless of the animals here, possess vastly more of the knowledge you admire than do either of us, yet they have no interest in it and continue to live in a wild condition."

Eliot's thoughts were returning to Alanie and the disinterest all the aliens had shown in her horrifying death. He remembered Balbain's enigmatic remark. "Abrak," he said bleakly, "what was *he* seeking?"

"His species craves *abnormal death.* The cause of it is thuswise: life, however long, must end. Life, then, is conditioned by death. Hence death is larger than life. Abrak's people are conscious that everything, ultimately, is abnegated by death, and they look for fulfilment only in the manner of their dying. An individual of his species seeks to die in some unusual or noteworthy manner. Suicides receive praise, provided the method is extraordinary. Murderers, likewise, are folk heroes, if their killings show imagination. Ultimately, the whole species strives to be exterminated in some style so extraordinary as to make its existence seem meaningful. Five seemed to offer that promise—not in its present state, it is true, but after suitable evolutionary development, perhaps due to an invasion by Abrak's people."

"And *you,*" Eliot demanded. "What do *you* seek?"

"We," answered Zeed with an icy lack of hesitation, "seek NULLITY. Not merely to die, like Abrak's species, but to wipe out the past, *never to have been.*"

Eliot shook his head, aghast. "How can *any* living creature have an ambition like that?"

"You must understand that on your planet conditions have been remarkably gentle and favorable for the arising of life. Such is not the general rule. Elsewhere there is hardship and struggle, often of a severity you could not imagine. The universe rarely smiles on the formation of life. On my planet . . ." Zeed seemed to hesitate, "we regard it as an act of compassion to kill our offspring at birth. The unlucky ones are spared to answer nature's call to perpetuate the species. If you knew my planet, you would not think that life could evolve there at all. We believe that ever since the first nervous system developed the subconscious feeling that it has all been a mistake has been present. To you, of course, it looks weird and perverted."

"Yes . . . it does indeed," Eliot said slowly. "In any case, isn't it impossible? I presume you are travelling the galaxy in search of some race that has time travel, so that you can wipe out your own past. But look at it this way: even if you succeeded in that, there would still have to be a 'different past'—the old past, a ghost past—in which you still existed."

"Once again you display your mental agility," Zeed said. "Your reasoning is sound: it may be that our craving can be satisfied only if the universe in its entirety is nullified."

Springing to his feet, Eliot went to the viewscreen and peered out on to turbulent, lightning-struck Five. He thought of Alanie and himself slaving in the laboratory, and felt tricked and insignificant. Zeed seemed to think of their work as no more than the collector's instinct of a jackdaw or an octopus.

"Everything you've told me passes for psychosis back in Solsystem," he said finally. "I don't know . . . maybe this is really a travelling lunatic asylum. You could all be insane, even by the standards of your own people. Balbain had this kinky desire to be a slave, Abrak wanted to be killed bizarrely, and you want never to have been born at all. What kind of a set-up is that? If you ask me, the normal, healthy, human mentality is a lot closer to reality than all that."

"Every creature says that of itself. It is hard for you to accept that your outlook is not a norm, that it is an aberration, an exception. Let me tell you how it arose. Because of the incredibly luxurious conditions on the planet Earth there was able to develop a quite unique biological class: the *mammalia*. The specific ethological feature of the mammalia is *protectiveness*, which began within the family, then extended to the tribe, and finally, with your own species, has become so over-developed as to embrace the whole of the mammalian class. Every mammal is protected, by your various organizations, whether human or not. Now, the point is that within this shield of protectiveness qualities are able to evolve which actually are quite redundant, since they bear no relation to the hard facts of survival. One of these, becoming intense among monkeys, apes and hominids, is playful curiosity, or meddlesome inquisitiveness. This developed into the love of knowledge which became the overriding factor in the history of your own species."

"That doesn't sound at all bad to me," Eliot said defensively. "We've done all right so far."

"But not for long, I fear. Your species is in more trouble than you think. There is no future in this mammalian over-protectiveness. The dinosaurs thought themselves safe by reason of their excessive size, did they not? And yet that giantism was exactly what doomed them. Already you ran into serious trouble when your compulsive care for the unfit led to a deterioration of the genetic stock. You saved yourselves that time because you learned to eliminate defective genes artificially. But perhaps other consequences of this nature of yours will arise which you cannot deal with. I do not anticipate that your species will last long."

"While you—death-lovers—will still be here, I suppose?"

Zeed's golden eyes seemed to dim and tarnish. "We all inhabit a vast dark," he repeated, "in which there is neither rhyme nor reason."

"Perhaps so." Eliot's fists were clenched now. "Here's another 'ethological feature', as you call it—revenge! Do you understand that, Zeed? I'm going to take my revenge for the death of my mate! I'm going out there to destroy the animal that killed Alanie."

Zeed did not answer but continued to stare at him and, so it seemed to Eliot's crazed imagination, lost any semblance to a living creature at all. Eliot ran to the lower galleries of the ship and armed himself with one of the few weapons the vessel carried: a high-powered energy beamer. As he stepped down from the ship and on to the booming, crashing surface of Five some of Zeed's words came back to him. An image came to his mind of the endlessness of space in which galaxies seemed to be descending and tumbling, and the words: *an unfathomable darkness without any common ground.* Then he pressed forward to challenge *Dominus.*

Dominus believed he had at last solved a perplexing riddle.

Following his initial seizure of one of the organisms, two others had emerged at short intervals so he had taken those also. A little later, he had moved in on the construct itself and taken a fourth organism from it. Of the fifth, there was no trace.

His analyses came up with the same result every time. The specimens were incomplete organisms: they were sterile. More accurately, they could only reproduce identical copies of themselves, like a plant.

Together with this, their tissues suffered from an inbuilt deficiency which caused them to decay with age.

Plainly these facts were not consistent with motile, autonomous entities. *Dominus* now believed that the specimens he had were only expendable doll-organisms, created by some genuine entity as one might make a machine to carry out certain tasks, and dispatched here, in the metal construct, for a purpose.

And that entity, the owner of the construct and of the doll-organisms, having intruded on his domain once, would be back again.

With that realization an urge beyond all power to resist came upon *Dominus*: the compulsion to *evolve.* He meditated in the depths of his being, and the entity to which he ultimately gave birth, amid great explosions, agonies and devastations, was as far above him in ability as he had been above his immediate inferior.

The new *Dominus* immediately set about the defense of his planet. The whole of the single continent became a spring-board for this defense, criss-crossed with artifacts which meshed integrally with the space-borne artifacts ranging several light-years beyond the atmosphere. To crew this extensive system *Dominus* copied the methods of the invader and created armies of slave doll-organisms modelled on the enemy's own doll-organisms. And *Dominus* waited for the enemy to arrive.

Jacob's Bug

RICHARD POSNER

I, JACOB CLEMENS, am writing this—what shall I call it? Confession? *Apologia pro vita mea*? In other centuries, felons about to be hanged would recite long narrative ballads recounting their wicked lives, to the delight of the gathered audience. It occurs to me that this reference will confuse. You are not geared toward history. You do not comprehend the very concept of history. This is necessary, of course, to the central aims of the government, but still, it would help if I could ring in analogies drawn from *autre temps, autre mores*—or have I mixed my languages?

I have been a student of history for some time now. It began as a pastime, a hobby to relieve the tensions of my work. It grew into a passion. I would close the door to my study and wrap myself in the cloak of the past, immersing my portly body and weary brain in Norman conquest, Czarist terrors, pioneer trails. I was, in fact, reading old books—yes, I have books, it is one of the privileges of my position—when they came for me.

How do I classify this final statement, which I have wheedled permission to pen? Yes, pen, damn it, with a genuine antique ball-point pen, on paper, parsimoniously donated by the Museum of Social History. I must be brief, since the donation was small. But I refuse to dictate into a recorder, or to type my words on a microfilmer. That would have been useless. If I am to make a gesture, it must bear the suitable trappings.

I can't really consider this a letter of instruction to the public, because there is no need for instruction. I suppose it might be termed a confession, but I find it hard to know which sin I am confessing. I'm afraid. That much I'll concede. And I miss Sara, desperately, but Sara would not know me. And I miss the springy, lank body I possessed, the wealth of dark hair, the bright eyes, the hawk nose, the quick, ingratiating smile. I miss, most of all—and this is indeed ironic—the searing ambition that jinxed my digestion.

Ambition. Yes, it glowed in me like a fire, from my boyhood. I sold newspapers when very young. I lived in a minuscule town, where the snow fell in October and melted in April. I wakened in darkness, bundled into clothes, and delivered the morning gazette from a toy wagon, in freezing rain and pre-dawn chills, in snow. But I soon owned the route, and other small boys did the delivering. I was President of the General Organization in High School, and presided, smirking, at school dances; chummy with the principal, evilly convincing him to adopt a rule of "scholarship first" for the football team, so that brawny captains flunked and retreated in shame while I comforted their breastful molls. I was generally successful with women, I possessed a charm far beyond my years and was at times able to convince girls outside my town that I was much older, and, thus, more desirable.

In college, I excelled in business administration, my

chosen field. I was a track star as well, my supple form suited for sprints and hurdles. I thus collected my own molls. One of these was a dewy-eyed, willowy blonde named Sara Janeway, daughter of a prosperous banker. Sara was different. She was remarkably intelligent, she was pliant and loving, hardheaded and pragmatic. When, after a long and arduous wooing, she at last allowed me entry to her perfumed secrets, I felt not the thrill of conquest, but the humility of attainment. I knew I would marry her. I asked and she accepted. The military separated us for two years, while I wangled a cushy post in Germany, typing out order forms and heaving myself, dismal and bored, into the comforting arms of luscious frauleins. My release came and I married Sara within days. We moved into a small apartment in the West 70's of Manhattan while I found a job as junior executive in the investment firm of Rheem and Barrington.

Rheem and Barrington guided moneyed gentry into tax shelters and eased corporations into immunity. They were eager and new when I joined the firm, but I suspected that they would grow. I chose Walter Rheem, the thin, pinched-faced nephew of the boss, as the man likely to succeed, and wooed him shamelessly. In fact, I was supporting him in a bitter little altercation with Clovis Jennings when the flu struck.

Clovis Jennings was immediately hateful to me, from my first day at work. She was a handsome, doe-eyed girl with shaggy brunette hair and a perverse temperament. She was, of course, conscious of being a woman in a man's business and overcompensated by a propensity for argument. Not that Walter Rheem was a prize. He simpered and snickered, leered and fleered, huffed and bluffed. He wore dark three-piece suits and slicked his thinning hair back with vaseline. He had a rather unappetizing skin condition. But I knew he was destined to inherit the business, and that he would at once fire Clovis if she were not already gone by then. So I hitched my wagon to the reigning star.

"Clovis," Rheem said that day—a rainy December day, full of chills and coughs—"I think my uncle knows what's best for this company. And believe me, diversification of the kind you suggest isn't a hot idea."

Clovis stood before Rheem's desk, pad in her small hands. She reddened—rather prettily. "I think you're small-minded," she said. "If I were a man, you'd consider my idea."

"That has nothing to do with it," Rheem said airily, turning his face aside to surreptitiously pick his nose. "We're an investment firm, and we have no desire to diversify."

"Not even for profit?" Clovis demanded. "If we acquire the Anderson Company, we'll have a top pharmaceutical outfit, and with our assets and management skills, we'll compete with the top companies for both government and public patronate. We can become powerful, Walter."

"No," Rheem said. "And if you persist, Clovis, I'll have to take it up with my uncle."

I had been waiting to see Rheem about another matter and I saw and heard the argument. Clovis turned to me, eyes snapping. "What do you think, Jacob?"

I was hesitant before answering; Clovis possessed a strong personality, a kind of charisma. But I looked away from her and said, "I must agree with Walter. We should keep our interests pure."

Rheem smirked. "Thank you, Jacob."

Clovis eyed me with bewilderment and sadness, then flounced out of the office. I congratulated myself and started into Rheem's office. The chills racked me as I stepped over the threshold, and the fever swirled through my head. Rheem blurred behind his desk, spun, and I scrabbled for support. I saw the blurred Rheem stand, and I saw the lush carpeting rushing up at my face.

"The bug," Dr. Zane said. "Definitely the bug. Jacob, you have the French flu."

Dr. Harry Zane was a new face. Sara had phoned Dr.

Percy, our regular physician, but Dr. Zane had arrived instead. "Dr. Percy is away," he'd said. "I'm covering his patients."

This was odd, since Dr. Percy had not mentioned anything about a vacation, but we were happy to get a doctor to come to the apartment. Dr. Zane was jolly, balding, red-cheeked, and stout. He smoked a pipe and chuckled a great deal. He was a youngish man, despite his lack of hirsute adornment, and he had a kind of old-school-tie camaraderie that was pleasant, if unnerving at times.

He folded his stethoscope and stuffed it into his black leather bag. I lay in bed, my convolutions stilled—as is always the case—by the arrival of the doctor. But I felt weak and moribund. Rheem had sent me home in a cab and I barely staggered up the two flights of stairs and scratched on the door before collapsing. Sara had fortunately come home from her graduate courses at NYU and screamed effectively when she saw me. She dragged me to bed and I'd been violently ill since that point. Now, Dr Zane produced a packaged syringe and tore it open.

"I'm going to give you a shot," he said. "That should help you rest."

Sara stood in the doorway, her arms folded nervously. "What is the French flu, doctor?" she asked.

Zane chuckled. "A puzzler, I'll tell you that. It seems to have come out of Marseilles, but nobody knows where it bred. It's a bug, like the Hong Kong flu, the Asian flu, the London flu. It's violent and strikes swiftly, producing a harsh illness. It's terribly contagious. Other than that, we're at a loss. Doctors are studying the disease, trying to isolate it, find a vaccine." He smiled becomingly. "I'm doing some research in that area myself."

"A G.P. who does research?" I asked hoarsely.

Dr. Zane's eyes narrowed and he assumed a haunted, fevered look. "I am a G.P. only to put bread in my stomach, Jacob. Research is my love. I intend to become a very powerful man. I am working in areas that terrify other medical men."

145 | *JACOB'S BUG*

The mask fell away abruptly and he was his jolly self. "Sleep, Jacob," he said, rising. "I'll drop by to see you again."

I listened to the reassuring murmurs of the doctor speaking with Sara, and I began to relax, the pains shooting less harrowingly through my body. Sara returned alone after the door slammed and she sat next to me, stroking my forehead, my damp hair.

"I feel so helpless when you're ill," she said softly.

I looked beyond her, transported by an excitement born of today's events. "Rheem likes me," I whispered. "Really likes me. I have a chance, Sara, to go all the way. We'll get out of this rathole and buy a house. We'll be wealthy. I swear it."

Sara's eyes clouded. "You're never away from the office, Jacob. Never with me. Is it always going to be this way? Are you always going to be driven, obsessed?"

I clenched a fist. "Until I get what I want. Yes."

The coolness of her hand was gone. I sensed her despair and I experienced a pang of remorse. But that was gone also. The room was dark and I floated, borne on the serum in my veins. I was frightened and joyful all at once.

I was walking through a long, alien corridor, the walls glowing softly. I had no memory of where I started from or where I was going. I felt stuffed, uncomfortable, completely off-balance. I looked at myself and was overcome with horror. I was huge; my stomach protruded alarmingly and my hands were puffy and old. I was dressed in a silvery tunic and loose fitting trousers and my feet were encased in silver slippers. The material looked harsh and metallic, yet felt airy against my skin. I found it a labor to breathe. I lurched forward, nearly fell against the wall.

A figure stepped out in front of me, seemingly from the wall itself. She was a fine, handsome woman with silver gray hair swept back to three peaks in a hairdo I'd never seen. She wore a violet eyeshadow, a gold lipstick, and a whitish cheek color. She also wore silver, in a formfitting suit that emphasized her lush figure. She was not a young woman at all; late middle age at least, yet she was marvelously preserved, alluring.

"Jacob," she said petulantly. "I haven't got all day."

"Sorry," I mumbled, trying to find my bearings.

I waddled—there is no other word for it—to her and followed her through a shimmering archway into a vast office. The room was done in ruby red, but the carpeting —what I thought was carpeting—was actually the floor itself, a yielding, warm material that was almost sexual in its texture. The furniture floated above the floor, a sweeping desk and molded chairs, and rather than walls, there was curved glass that looked out on a jewelled, incredible city. Spires vied with towering blocks, sunlight made deep blue shadows, shapes changed, glass facades shattered the light into blinding fragments. I was overwhelmed by the sight, and yet, it made sense. Everything made sense, only I couldn't remember. I wasn't shocked by these sights, only unbalanced. I knew, instinctively, that I belonged here.

"Well, sit down," the woman said. "You've been acting strangely for a week now, Jacob. Are you ill?"

"No," I said, trying not to say too much.

She took the chair behind the desk and I realized I could not feel the seat on which I rested. It was as if I floated also. The sensation was comforting, allowing me to forget the elephantine proportions of my body. The woman looked harshly at me and I stared, in turn, at her. There was something about her face, even beneath the grotesque makeup, that pricked me. I struggled to remember, and the name came to me in a rush, nearly causing me to faint.

"Clovis," I whispered.

She cocked an eyebrow. "Well, success at last. You know my name. I'm delighted, Jacob, simply delighted. Would you like to try your ABC's?"

"You're Clovis," I said.

She was suddenly concerned. "Yes, I'm Clovis. Jacob, did you honestly forget?"

"Where am I?" I pleaded, suddenly full of fear. "Where is this place? Why am I fat? Why do you look like that?"

She half rose. "Jacob, sit right there, I'm going to get the doctor for you. Obviously, you're not well."

She stood up and stepped lithely to the floor. I stood also, though I very nearly fell. I stopped her, a hand on her shoulder. "Clovis, you've got to give me some answers."

Her eyes were full of compassion. "Jacob. You do remember your name?"

"Yes," I said eagerly. "Jacob Clemens. And you're Clovis Jennings."

She shook her head. "No. Just Clovis now. I am the regent for Hemisphere. And you are Vice Regent. We are two of the most powerful people in the Western World, and you were to report to me today on your efforts to annex South America to our empire. You were at work on a savagely complex business deal, involving the extermination of native insurgents, the transference of bank funds, the floating of bonds. Jacob, don't you remember any of this?"

I stood helplessly, my hands outspread. "No."

She took a deep breath. "All right. You might have fallen, jarred your head. It's nothing the doctor can't handle. Perhaps the strain of business, the pressures of power. It can happen."

I tightened my hand on her shoulder. "Where's Sara?"

She narrowed her eyes, "Sara? You mean the girl you once married?"

"Yes, Sara, my wife."

"Jacob, she hasn't been your wife for years. Not since 1975. That's when the divorce became final. You do recall the divorce, don't you? Naming me as correspondent. Following our rather torrid little affair?"

She smiled hopefully. I moistened my lips. "No, I don't remember a divorce. I'm still married to her. And it's not 1975 yet."

She gently disengaged herself from my grip and I detected a ripple of fear in her expression. "Listen carefully, Jacob. The year is 2003. You are 59 years old. I am 57. And Sara is out there somewhere among the masses. We lived together for twenty-six years before our positions became too demanding for emotion to cloud the work. We rule what once was the United States, Canada, Mexico, Central America, and after your current work, most of South America. We are in a fatal struggle with Africa and the Orient for domination of Europe. We must win the battle or we stand to fall to the combined black and yellow empires, utterly wiped out. We cannot allow that to happen. With South America in our pockets, we have bargaining power. Europe needs South America, and so will need us. We can arrange a deadlocked trade agreement that will wipe out the black and yellow threat. Is this coming back to you, darling?"

I shivered, my head full of alien images. Rebelling peasants crushed by flying saucers, except the saucers were ours. Huge business conferences held at the summits of Mt. Everest and the bottom of the Pacific Ocean. Insane, impossible images.

"Will there be war?" I asked, trying to grope for answers. "Atomic war?"

She grasped my hands. "No, Jacob. Nuclear weapons were disarmed years ago. The shift in temperature, gravity, air quality. The ecological upheavals. The physical reactions that produced atomic explosions no longer exist. The stockpiles are useless. We have the rays, of course, the handweapons, the tanks and aircraft, but a war fought with those would be endless and useless. We fight with commerce now. We use contracts as bombs. Think, Jacob, and you'll remember. You and I were instrumental in making it happen. We annexed the Anderson Company, and, with the doctor's skills, we produced the miracle drugs, and Compound 15. We secured the government contracts and built our power until we were the biggest multinational conglomerate. We were there when the black fogs wiped out Chicago and Los Angeles, when New

York was shattered by the Street Wars. We discovered how to use waste materials as fuel, we had the means to save the world. We sold it at outrageous prices, gaining complete control. We bought out the other companies. But the black and yellow empires prospered also, neck and neck with us in biological attainment, strong with mastery of yoga. Ruthless, unafraid to lose millions to win. They learned the ropes, learned commerce from Japan. Jacob, I want you to get well."

She hurried from the office, seeming to diffuse into the wall and disappear. I gaped after her, alone in the vast office. I spun slowly, taking it all in, beginning to sense my worth, my power. I owned this. With Clovis, I ruled. I felt invincible, heady. My brain was filled with bubbles. I laughed.

"It wasn't a dream," I told Dr. Zane, struggling for the energy to speak. The afternoon sunlight splashed the bedroom, as I lay in a pool of perspiration. Sara was in the living room, weeping. Dr. Zane leaned close to me, his eyes aglow.

"Yes?" he urged.

"I've had dreams," I said. "I know they can be vivid. I know they can be mistaken for reality. I've even had dreams of waking from dreams. I know all about it. But this was no dream. I was in the future. I travelled to the year 2003 and I was the ruler of the world. Is this insanity?"

"It might be," Dr. Zane said. "Could you accept that?"

I turned away, bitter. "I don't know. I don't think so. Not after that vision. I was, in the office, a magnificent office, with Clovis Jennings, and she was the queen of everything. I couldn't remember my life from now until then, but she remembered it. Somehow I got there, and I want to go back. I want to see it again. If it was a fever dream, I want to live in it. It was the culmination of my ambition."

Dr. Zane placed a restraining hand on my arm. "Easy,"

he said. "You still have the flu. It won't do you any good to become excited. It's very possible you had a dream, a particularly vivid one. If so, you have to accept that."

I eyed him shrewdly. "You're not humoring me, as I would have expected. You haven't committed yourself. You think there's another possibility."

He seemed to look into himself, to make a great decision. He pursed his lips, tapped on his black leather bag. "Yes," he said, finally. "I think there is another possibility. Among other things, I've always believed in the possibility of time travel. I couldn't explain the physics to you, but the universe is too patterned to rule it out. Time is only another dimension, and dimensions can be crossed. It is possible you journeyed in time, Jacob. You realize you can never quote me, not to anybody, because I will deny it."

"Of course," I said. "But listen. I can appreciate travelling backward in time. The past happened, after all. But the future hasn't happened yet. How can I visit a place that doesn't exist, that won't exist for decades?"

Dr. Zane clucked. "I don't know, Jacob. I have theories. Time might well be a belt, a loop. Who is to say that time is a straight line, a continuing series of events leading to infinity? Perhaps everything has already happened, and will only happen again. Perhaps earth will reach a stage where it will explode, or wither and freeze under a dead sun, and perhaps eons will pass after that, and the sun will be reborn, the earth molten, then seas, dinosaurs, prehistoric man, the entire sequence of events, over and over again, an endless cassette. In that case, Jacob, your future does indeed exist, and has existed and will exist again. These moments will occur an infinite number of times, and you will live infinite lives. If this is true, Jacob, then you simply travelled along the belt to another notch."

I was desperately excited. I raised myself slightly on the pillow. "All right. But how? I have no time machine."

Dr. Zane chuckled, clamped his pipe between his teeth, squinted as the sun struck his glasses. "We are so machine-conscious. Computers, assembly lines. Naturally, we would assume that time travel, like auto or air travel, must be accomplished in a mechanical conveyance, replete with buttons and levers. But why? We already know that the human mind is capable of vast experience. We have barely tapped the surface. Drugs, yoga, occult happenings have shown us places and ways beyond the capacities of machines. We thought we were medical messiahs until the orientals showed us accupuncture. Our minds simply need a catalyst to take off, to soar. Perhaps your mind experienced such a catalyst, and was released."

"What catalyst?" I asked.

Zane's eyes glittered. "I don't know, Jacob. But the bug —the French flu—is still unexplored. We don't know what it will do."

"Are you suggesting that the flu enabled me to travel through time?"

"Not suggesting, merely raising the ghost of the possibility."

"But this flu is epidemic. Others have had it."

"No two systems are the same, Jacob. What affects one will not affect another. I have often been stung by bees. A moment of pain, then nothing. Yet a patient of mine died in grotesque agony four minutes after such a sting. Our bodies are not the same."

I seized his wrist. "Then inject me with more of the flu. Let me go back."

He shook his head. "It's no good, Jacob. You live here and now. The you that lives in 2003 is already there. That's why you could not remember anything, why you felt off balance. Two of you inhabited the same time, the same place. It can't happen. You must live your life and become the you of 2003. Suffice it that you had a glimpse, a privilege that few men have. You might use the glimpse to revise your life accordingly."

He snapped shut his bag and stood. "I think you're well on the road to recovery, Jacob. I won't be dropping in again."

He left the room and I lay back, exhausted, yearning fiercely for the world I had just left.

That night, Sara lay beside me, rippling the pages of a magazine. I stared into space, preoccupied. The flu was abating, and my strength was beginning to surge again. I had eaten a healthy supper this evening, and I knew that by the beginning of next week, I could return to work.

Sara lay the magazine aside and turned to me, the bed creaking as she did so. Outside the frosted window, the clatter of New York at Christmastime penetrated the walls. The steam clanked and made the apartment stifling. Sara moved to me and kissed my neck.

"I'm sorry I was cross with you before," she said.

"No apologies are needed."

She must have sensed my coolness. "You have to understand, darling. It seemed so horrid to me. The way you thrashed in a coma and insisted you'd travelled in time. I thought you were delirious."

"I can see why."

She held my wrist with both her hands and I could feel the warmth of her body. "I don't want to be gone from your life," she said. "I sometimes feel as if I live with a stranger, but I love you all the same."

I patted her hands. "I know. I love you too."

"Do you, Jacob? I hope you do."

"Of course I do."

She arched her body and kissed me again. "I hate this flu bug," she hissed.

I mumbled a reply. Already I was thinking of my strategy at work.

I was greeted heartily at work when I returned the following Monday, a brash, windy day. Clovis glared at me when I passed her desk and I forced a smile and said good morning.

"Well, you're cheerful today," she said frostily.

"I feel better. And you look very lovely."

She raised an eyebrow. "Thank you."

I stared at her and tried to superimpose the fascinating woman with the silver hair and the gold lipstick. It was the same woman, much transformed, but Clovis, this raggedy, pretty, pouting young girl. I felt an odd tingle, as if I were half in one world and half in the other.

Rheem came prancing from his office, his slender hand grasping a manila folder. He stopped and smiled silkily at me, brushing back his oiled hair.

"How do you feel, Jacob?" he asked.

"Better."

"Good. That flu is a nasty thing."

"Sure is, Walter."

"Oh," Rheem said. "I thought you'd want to know; I've officially killed the Anderson deal. Told them to go sing. I knew you'd be happy to hear it."

He glanced significantly at Clovis, who turned away, frustrated. I took a deep breath, praying, and said, "I'm sorry to hear that, Walter. It's probably the dumbest thing you've ever done."

He looked as if he'd been shot point blank. "What?"

"You heard me. Clovis was absolutely right and I was an idiot to ignore it. You're a slimy incompetent, getting along on your uncle's misplaced good will, and you should be in the mail room. Clovis, if anyone, should be managing director, and probably will be, and I intend to be at her side."

Clovis was goggling at me, her mouth open as if the hinge had snapped. Rheem turned bright red and blustered. "All right, Clemens," he gargled when he finally found his voice. "I see how it stands. A pretty face counts for more than good sense. Very well. You and Clovis may enjoy yourselves. But I'm afraid it's both of you who will be in the mail room when the dust clears."

He turned on his elevated heel and flounced away while I stood shuddering. Clovis stood and laid a hand on my arm. "I don't understand this," she said softly. "But I'm grateful for the support."

"Just good business," I said hoarsely. "I honestly think you'll be in a position of power someday, and I want to be there with you."

She smiled dazzlingly. "Jacob, I've been a little in love with you since I came here. If I achieve anything in my life, you'll be there with me. I promise you that."

I gulped. I felt a new passion coursing through my blood, a romantic ardor that I'd lost with Sara. I heard myself ask Clovis to join me for lunch, and I heard her say yes.

"But you really shouldn't be too close to me," she said. "My brother has the French flu and I've been exposed. You might have a relapse."

I smiled before I took her in my arms and stopped smiling as I kissed her. She was surprised, to say the least, but not unwilling.

I was in my study, as I said earlier, leafing through old novels when I heard the clatter: Three regal guards, in full uniform, and Clovis, and Dr. Zane. An old, white-tufted Dr. Zane, with translucent skin, his eyes still glittering. Somehow, I was not surprised to see him, and I was not lost.

"What's wrong?" I asked.

Clovis was crying, and it unnerved me. She'd always been so strong, so invulnerable. She shook her head. "I'm so sorry, Jacob. So terribly sorry."

"It all checks out, Jacob," Dr. Zane said. "You've travelled in time at least twice now."

I stood, eager, angry at my corpulence. "Yes, I know. I just arrived back here now. I made love to Clovis—the young Clovis—when she'd been exposed to the flu. I caught it again and I fainted on the subway coming home. It must have just happened."

Clovis smiled bravely. "I remember, Jacob. I remember the first time we made love. You were very strong."

She looked queenly and unattainable as she turned away. "Yes," Dr. Zane said, nodding. "It was the flu bug. We thought so. The French flu. That ancient disease. But it was the making of me, when I found the antidote, the cure, and from the cure evolved Compound 15. You know about Compound 15, don't you Jacob?"

I felt uneasy, suddenly afraid. "Yes," I said, surprised that I did know. "The contentment drug."

"Exactly," Dr. Zane agreed. "Introduced to water supplies, it induced passivity, destroyed resistance, individuality. We got to all the radicals, all the revolutionaries, because they all drank water, and the job was done before it was too late. It enabled you and Clovis to rise to power, enabled this day to dawn."

"Brainwashing," I said, suddenly, and with vehemence. "You brainwashed everybody. Even Sara—"

"Yes, of course," Zane said petulantly. "She's out there with the bovine masses. You never did like it, Jacob. You had that nasty streak of righteousness that only surfaced recently. Your ambition spent, you turned to history, to romanticism, and now you're dangerous. Very dangerous."

"What can I do?" I said bitterly. "Un-brainwash them? I'm no mad scientist, Zane."

"No," he said, evenly. "But the French flu affected your body so oddly. It enabled you to travel in time."

"Yes," I said, placing my hands on the work book, looking at Clovis. "Yes, it enabled me to travel to the future, as you theorized, and to see this horror."

Zane laughed, so oddly that I was forced to look at him.

"Fool," Zane snapped. "It's impossible to travel to the future. The future hasn't happened. I see you fell for my gobbledegook at your bedside. I was young and naive then. I had silly theories."

He gestured to the guards, who approached me with guns drawn. The horror was already upon me. "You carried that bug in you for years," Zane said. "It did nothing. Until now. Until it incubated and you began to travel in time. Not to the future, Jacob. To the past. Where you first caught the flu. You didn't glimpse this future, Jacob, you remembered it. You'll probably travel again, and you'll remember even more. Until you remember all of it and you don't follow the script. Is it clear now?"

They bound me and I struggled to comprehend, stared at Clovis. "You had to take the first trip," Zane said slowly. "Because you remembered enough to change your tune with Clovis. To court her, to help her rise to power, with your talent. If you hadn't taken the first trip, we would not be here now. You made this world, Jacob. Because of your little bug. We thank you for that. I was delighted when Clovis went for me, told me of your blackout in her office. It meant we were set. You'd gone back. You'd made the move."

"But," he said, as Clovis came to me. "We can't allow you to go again, Jacob. Because of this righteousness, this dislike of our methods. If you remember too much, you'll desert Clovis at a critical point, prevent this all from happening. We can't allow that. We can't let you depose us, because, you see, you *do* have that power. We have to kill you, Jacob. It's the only way. I'm sorry."

Clovis held my hand. I thought of Sara and what my ambition had done to me, to the world. And then I screamed.

I'm out of paper now, so this confession must end. It can't do any good because, as far as I know, I'm the only one who was affected by the bug in this way. And now I can't go back again. They're watching me. They'll kill me instantly if I begin to black out, rather than wait for the official execution and risk my changing the future. So it's a lost cause.

Perhaps this will serve as instruction, then, after all. I said I was a recent student of history. Well, this is the most concise history of the modern world that you'll ever read. And the most accurate.

Getting Around

K. M. O'DONNELL

I

—I would very much like to have sex with you and think that we've reached that point of our relationship where it's become inevitable.

—So do I.

—But before we begin, I'm afraid I have a confession to make and no getting around it. You see, I have no penis.

—Oh.

—Yes, I was born that way.

—Well, that's nothing to be so terribly ashamed of. Medical science is doing wonderful things nowadays; progress is being made in many areas. Perhaps you could—

—Oh, you're right about medical science. Until three years ago I had no arms and legs, six months ago I had no vocal cords. They're putting me together step by step as you can see. But they haven't tackled the penis problem yet. They say I'm not ready for that yet. Maybe in a little while. . . .

—Oh, I'm sure they will! Doctors are *so* wonderful!

—In the meantime, I can offer you oral sex, manual sex, polymorphous perverse sex . . . oh, many things. I hope that will be satisfactory.

—It sounds just right.

—I'm so glad that I told you this rather than having you discover it on your own.

—I'm glad too. You mean you were born without arms, legs, and vocal cords?

—Yes.

—You must have had a very unhappy childhood.

—Oh no. You see, I didn't have a brain either.

—Now I'm excited. I'm *really* excited.

—Let's go to the bedroom.

II

Dear Lucinda: I know that this letter will do me no good and that writing you in this way is an infantile gesture and yet, somehow, I cannot control myself even though at this moment I hear your calm, reasonable voice saying as you look at me out of those penetrating eyes, "Herbert, you're making a very bad mistake. Herbert, you're an emotional fool," and so I am, Lucinda, I am an emotional fool but nevertheless looking at you across the room at the Intermix again last night, seeing you in the arms of others, your body open and sprawling before them (as it had opened and sprawled before *me* at the Intermix before) I could not somehow, and this must be faced squarely so I will face it, could not somehow escape strong feelings of *jealousy* and *desire* because I wanted you very much Lucinda and was hurt to know that since I was not in your assigned group last night I could not have you.

I know better than you do the pointlessness of these feelings and how more than anything else they must work against the *spirit* of the Intermix which is liberation through exposition to various levels of contact and partner (I can quote this jargon even better than you might think being, as you know, a copywriter) but nevertheless I feel impelled to give you these feelings straight out because one of the other lessons of the Intermix is the *freeness and openness* between persons as a result of the experience and how can I be free and open with you, my beloved Lucinda, if I sit upon this well of feeling which was opened by seeing you held by others whose delight I could not share since I was not last night a member of your activity group?

Well, there is no way for you to answer this, Lucinda, no way whatsoever, what has to be faced as well (and even in my misery I counsel my own openness and hence will face it) is that you are not terribly bright my dear: an impulsive being who lives very close to your emotional surfaces and their immediate response you lack the capacity for pain which I feel Lucinda and doubtless have very little idea of what I am talking about.

But just this then, saying just this: looking at you across the room, held by another (I do not recall her name; a pleasant, heavy suffering girl who lives on the lower western section of the city I believe and who I have seen a few times at Intermix although never so intimately) I felt pain the dimensions of which I will not explain to you and the rising of an ancient, almost absent desire, something that I thought did not exist any more, it was the desire to have you exclusively for my own in some world where Intermix did not exist and where we could lie on fields, say, green fields inhabited by grass and sheep, we would hold one another and roll on that grass, overcome by the evil design of possession and in this world where Intermix did not exist I would not have to share you and in my unseemly need for you this image cajoled me over the edge and before I quite knew what had happened I had dumped into this pleasant, heavy girl a vast suffering load drawn from me not into *her* but into some image of *you*; I know that there is no hope for me, Lucinda, I know that there is no hope whatsoever but I found myself unable to stay away from this letter and if only I can gain the courage I will drop it through the delivery chute and what will you say, what will you *say* when you read it; no I cannot go on this way, "Herbert you are a fool," I hear your admonition now and saying no more, knowing that I am indeed a fool I will only instead dispose of this and

III

NOTES FOR ORIENTATION LECTURE (copyright © 1981; unauthorized use or duplication strictly prohibited):

a) Post-technological era; shift of culture toward consumption-orientation.

b) Love ideal as culture lag; love ideal linked to pre-consumption culture in which *denial* was celebrated.

c) Need for new ethic in post-technological consumption-oriented culture. More in tune with times.

d) Goal-oriented behaviorism. History, cf.: Skinner.

e) Historical roots of Intermix: Encounter, group sex as primitive efforts. Lack of systematization.

f) The need to systematize as the key to post-technological relationships and thinking.

g) Huber, 1975 and the Code of Intermix. The history of Huber, early defeats, misunderstandings, hostility as evidences of culture lag.

h) The heroism of Huber, fight against establishment, Skinnerian ideal versus Freudian cant. How it prevailed.

i) Establishment of the Institute, the acceptance of Intermix.

j) Early versions of Intermix: homosexuality, multiple sexual behavior, animal perversions. Superseded in the search for the heterosexual ethic.

k) The establishment of the heterosexual ethic.

l) Present success of Intermix, acceptance of the Institute, Intermix as goal-directed behavior, as healthful and supersession of neuroses. Etc.

m) Possible future of Intermix. Eastern cultures, pre-technological cultures, polygamous cultures, the adaptation of the code.

n) Intermix and religion.

IV

—I feel so terribly awkward.

—Just relax.

—You see, it's my very first time here; previously I—

—There must be a first time for everyone. Just relax.

—I was a monogamist for many years until my wife and I had a misunderstanding. . . .

—You had a wife? How amusing.

—That's how I feel about it.

—What a strange sect! I knew you looked terribly quaint when you came through the door.

—Well yes, yes. I make no excuses of course, it's all completely my own fault.

—Come here you strange little man.

—I'm a little frightened and nervous. But I *am* responding. There! Can't you see I'm responding?

—Of course you are. I always knew you would.

—I'm glad that they gave me a specialist for my first time.

—Well, of course. Yes you can do that. Ah! Do it more, more, more.

—My wife always liked that too. She said . . .

—Don't say anything about your wife! You must not mention your wife! Do you want to ruin everything?

—No, of course not.

—Then concentrate on the present. In Intermix you live in present time. Intermix destroys the past and future and uses the ingredients in the timeless present. That is the theory. There! You're doing much better.

—Thank you.

—You'll do even better than that if you'll just close your eyes.

V

Dear Lucinda: Last night although it has been several weeks, perhaps I am thinking of months, since you switched from the group and I last saw you I found myself thinking of you again and try as I could to combat the image, that sudden, shrieking, poisonous image of you which rose before my eyes like a sheet, staring at me bland and expressionless, eyes dense with knowledge, try as I could to combat that image as I said I found myself hopelessly battering at it, moving my way as if on a staircase of feeling higher and higher against you and at the moment of climax with a partner I cannot even remember now (how dark glows my sin!) it was into you I came, into you blessed Lucinda and now I know truly that I am damned for after the session I did not as proper render full explanation and appreciation to my partner(s) but instead rushed from the Intermix in awkward haste and silence, stumbling down corridors, your face shrieking its way through my being as I came back to these rooms and even at this moment I cannot forget you, I cannot eliminate this feeling, I know now that it is too late for me and realizing that if I were to mail this letter (I have never mailed you any of my letters) sure destruction would result for the two of us I want you to know that I am destroying this and then will take the capsules that will end my life.

Oh Lucinda, Lucinda, it was never to be but I will say it and be damned, say it and know the vengeance of Huber through a thousand centuries of afterlife, say it and then end: we should have been monogamous and I should have should have should have had you alone, but I know

VI

—I see that you've received your penis.

—Yes, I got it just today, isn't it beautiful? And it's guaranteed to work without fail ninety-nine times out of a hundred or they'll fix it for free. Forever.

—Oh, I'm so pleased for you! Are you complete now?

—Except for a few last touch-ups and details. They're going to put feeling in next Thursday.

The Answer

TERRY CARR

"WHAT WAS IT LIKE, being a man?" the alien asked Stan Nelsen.

It took a second or two for the words to penetrate Stan's mood. He had been sitting motionless in the Presidential Suite of the Statler Hilton for hours, staring at the floor while the sad, disconnected thoughts that he had become accustomed to lately traced their way through his mind.

He looked up at the light blue being from the stars who stood before him. The alien had dry, wrinkled skin with a fine down on all the portions not covered by his toga-like clothing. He stood nearly seven feet tall and had two large, multifaceted eyes, which rested patiently on Stan now, waiting for him to reply.

"I'm sorry," Stan said. "What did you ask me?"

"What was it like, being a man?" the alien asked again.

Stan frowned, somewhat annoyed at having his thoughts disturbed for idle questions. The aliens had been perfectly thoughtful, even solicitous, ever since they had found him amid the ruins of New York. After their initial questions they had left him alone when he wanted to be alone—which was just about always.

"I wasn't a man," Stan told the alien shortly. "I was still a boy, just fifteen years old."

The alien made a sound like a chuckle. "Then what was it like, being a boy just fifteen years old? I really want to know, Stan Nelsen. I've seen what's happened to the planet outside those windows—I want to know how that happened."

"I told you, all of you," Stan muttered. "There was a war, with bombs and nerve gases and then later the fall-out. It was all over before we ever heard your signals from space; there were only a couple dozen people still alive in New York then. And they all died before you got there. All but me."

The alien nodded, and the somewhat longer hairs on the top of his head rippled in a gesture Stan didn't understand. "You did tell us all that, but you didn't make us understand *why*. Obviously, the reason was in what men were, so I want to know what it was like to be one of them."

"I don't know," Stan said. "I never thought about it like that."

"Then please think about it now," the alien said. He moved over to one of the windows and stood looking out; beyond him Stan could see the jagged silhouettes of torn and broken buildings rising against a gray sky. Out there, he knew, were the crumbling remains of what had been the greatest city on Earth—dead and empty now.

He shook his head. How could he explain why men had started a war they had known would kill the entire race? He didn't know why himself.

"What was it like, Stan Nelsen?" the alien asked once more, turning from the window.

Stan stood up. "Come out into the city with me," he said, "and I'll try to tell you a little about it."

They walked through what had been the heart of Manhattan—going slowly, pausing beside the remains of a department store, a movie theater, an art museum. They went through the seared grounds of Central Park, and Stan showed the alien where he had played baseball, on a field which was now only scorched earth; where he had rowed on a lake which had been turned to steam by the heat from the bomb over New Jersey, so that now there was only a dry depression in the ground, baked hard and cracked like an arid desert; where he had fed peanuts to squirrels and where he had seen bears and tigers in cages and where a bird had once turned a curious eye on him from a tree.

Then he told the alien what squirrels and bears and tigers and birds were, because there were no more of them left, just as there were no humans except for Stan.

When he had finished all this, the alien asked, "Was it all good, like the things you've told me about?"

Stan thought back, and shook his head slowly. "No," he said, and took the alien to a street corner where an old man had died in a soiled vest and with a bottle of wine in one hand; to another place where there had been a knife fight which Stan had watched with frightened fascination; to the building where a club Stan had belonged to had voted that they'd take Chinese kids as members, but not Negroes. Then he told the alien what different races were, and why some people thought they were important. He had trouble with the last part.

When they came back to the hotel, the alien said, "I think you've done your best to explain it all to me, Stan Nelsen. But there are too many contradictions. Good and evil side by side, sometimes in the same people; beauty and ugliness, lies and truth, strength and weakness, all mixed up together. This doesn't seem logical."

"I'd never thought much about it," Stan said slowly.

"But it's a funny thing—telling you about it, trying to help you understand, made me see it all for myself. All of a sudden, while we were walking around, I began to realize that what I was saying didn't make sense." He frowned. "But it was the truth, and I never saw it until today . . . until I saw it all through your eyes."

The alien looked at him for several seconds, his multi-faceted eyes shining in the evening sun. "No," he said. "You didn't see these things through my eyes. You saw them yourself, but you never thought about them. That was a mistake."

Stan nodded, looking around at fallen stones and girders, cracked and torn sidewalk, fire-blackened doorways. A vagrant breeze blew past, carrying with it the smell of decay and death which hung over the city now. It was an awfully big city to be so empty, he thought—and that was another contradiction for the alien.

"Yes, it was a mistake," he said. "But it was a mistake we all made, not seeing what was in front of us."

He paused, thinking. Then he added, "You asked me earlier what it was like to be a man. Well, I guess that's your answer. We made mistakes. All of us. We made mistakes."

In Outraged Stone

R. A. LAFFERTY

THE LOOK OF indignation on the face of that artifact was only matched by the total outrage of her whole figure. Oh, she was a mad one! She was the comic masterpiece of the Oganta Collection. If stone could speak she would be shrilling. She was a newly catalogued item among that grotesque alien stonery called the Paravata Oneirougma.

"You'd almost believe that she were alive!" was the laughing comment of many who watched her there in the display. "Oh, it's that she *was* alive once, and now she is furious at finding herself frozen in stone."

But that was the whole missed point of her outrage: she wasn't alive; and she never had been.

It was the cultural discovery time of the Oganta of Paravata. The Oganta had become things both in and interesting. Earth people had taken a seasonable delight in their rough culture, in their horniness, in their froggishness. Many earth people from the scientific simmer were now visiting them and studying them. In particular were those of the psychologic phratry involved in this. A quick trip to Paravata would yield such theses as enhance reputations and make names. There the mysterious human undermind and underbody was atop and open to explore. There was no way that one could miss if he had the energy for the encounter.

The energy for it, though: that was the thing that separated the bulls from the steers and the horned heifers from the freemartins.

"Paravata has half again earth's gravity, so it calls out our strength. It has an atmosphere that keeps one on an oxygen binge, so it gives that strength something to draw on," so had Garamask, that most vigorous earthman, said of the planet.

Many earth people wilted on Paravata. They couldn't stand the weight (there was something wrong about the weight) and the weirdness: they hadn't the strength for it. But others (and not always the ones you would guess) found a new strength and excitement there. It was bigger than life and rougher. It was vulgar and misshapen. It was a grinning challenge and it would smash anyone who wasn't up to it.

But if you could make it there you could make it big. The loins bulged with new energy for these fortunates, and the adrenalin ran in rivers. It was a common and shouting and delirious world for those who could match it, and it was not only the body juices that were called into fresh spate. The mind juices sang their new tunes also, and the ideas came in tumbling torrents. They were pretty shaggy, some of those ideas, but there was nothing tired about them. Mind and body appetites grew steeply, almost exploded. There was an absolute horniness that came onto such visitors as had the capacity to take it. And a froggishness. What is the mystique about frogs?

The horned frog of earth is a miserable sleepy little antediluvian and has nothing to do with these vigorous whorls. Let us take the name away from it and give it to another. Somewhere, on some world, there is a real horned frog, rampant with green comedy, outrageous in its assumptions, able to get away with worse than murder. The Oganta of Paravata were really such horned frogs, except that they hadn't actual visible horns, except that they were frogs only in a manner of speaking.

Five young earth psychologists (they all had the capacity and ruggedness for Paravata) were dining in one of those gape-walled inns on a ridge above the small town of Mountain Foot on one of the stunning Paravata plateaus. Dining wasn't the proper word for it: they were gorging. They were gorging with Oganta friends (an Oganta had to be your friend or one of you would be dead quickly). And they didn't sit at table for their stupendous eating. This would be unthinkable to the Oganta, and it was immediately unthinkable to the earth people. For such action, they stood, they strode, they rollicked; they tromped about on the big tables from giant bowl to giant bowl, and they grabbed and ate commonly from these common caldrons. They dipped and slurped, they toothed great joints of flesh-meat, they went muzzle-deep into musky mixtures. They were as mannerless as the Oganta themselves. They were already full of the coarse Oganta spirit and had even taken on something of the Oganta appearance.

On Paravata, one never reclined when he could stand (the Oganta even took their carnal pleasure leaping and hopping); one never sauntered where he could stride, nor walked when he could run. Aimless it all might be, but there was a burning energy and action in the very aimlessness.

They wrestled, they rolled, they walked upon one another and sat upon one another. "Och, I could hardly eat another bellyful," Margaret Mondo groaned happily as she rolled on one of the big tables among the bowls. Then a huge male Oganta landed in the middle of her belly with both feet and bounced. Ah, he'd have gone three hundred pounds on earth, and things were half again as heavy on Paravata. "Och, now I can eat again. How I can eat!" Margaret chortled. We knew that Margaret, the earthiest of them all, wouldn't really give out so quickly. The dining customs on Paravata are extreme. If you can't take them, don't go there.

It was just at frost-bite and there was a light snow sifting. The five youngish earth-folk were dressed near as barely as the Oganta. It would be many degrees colder than this before the walls of this mountain inn would be raised. The open air is always to be praised. On Paravata there were no heating fires ever, except the internal ones: and these burned hot.

"It's much more earthy than Earth," George Oneiron was saying, was almost shouting. "It's everything, it's all through everything. The butterflies here are absolutely rampant, they're rutting, they're ravening. We know that 'psyche' originally meant butterfly as well as soul. The psyche, the soul-mind-person, is our field of study, and here it is grossly material, fleshed and blooded. Even the Marsala Plasma of this place (there's no counterpart to it on Earth, there couldn't be), though it floats and drifts and jostles in the air, has a heaviness and materiality about it that startles one. Don't turn your back on one of those floating blobs or it'll crash down on you like nine tons of rock. We'll solve the mystery of these plasma balls, or we will not solve any other mystery here."

The Oganta themselves had this sometimes weightlessness and this sometimes great weight. It was a part of the jokes they played. And the earth people discovered that now they had it too, sometimes, mostly when they were in contact with the oafish Oganta. You are light or heavy when you think light or heavy.

The floating globs, the air balls, had more mysteries than their weight. There was their sound, the most raucous dissonance ever, when one caught it only out of the corner of the ear. But turn full ear on one, and it was all innocence and quiet. Incredible scenes flashed and lounged inside the balls when taken at a careless glance, but they murked over when looked at straight. The globs made lascivious gestures, but what was lascivious about them? They were only charged air drifting in uncharged air (if there was any uncharged air on Paravata). The lasciviousness must be in the eye of the beholder. But what were the globs anyhow? "Oh, they're persons, some of our own persons, persons that we're not using right now," one of the Oganta tried to explain it.

George Oneiron, still avid to solve the mystery, was trying to take one of these plasma balloons into his hands. It was a yellowish, greenish, translucent, transparent glob of crystal gas (crystal gas? yes, crystal gas) the size of his own head. It challenged him. It was as if it shook its horns at him. He had it, it escaped him, he had it again; he grunted and grappled with it, he seized it out of the shimmering air and he didn't seize it easily.

"It'll go heavy on you," one of the Oganta grinned. "It'll cut you to shreds. Its weight is polaroid, just as ours is, just as yours begins to be. If it's in alignment it hasn't any weight; if it isn't it's crushing. You match it or it breaks you down. You shape with it or one of you breaks to pieces."

George Oneiron was quite strong; and the thing, after all, was only a floating glob of gas. "I have you now!" he cried when he had it. "Why do you follow and cling to the Oganta while you evade ourselves? I have you, and you'll spill your secrets to me."

"Poor George is reduced to talking to globs of air," Helen Damalis jibed, but Helen was no great one at understanding deep things.

Actually, it was a giant wrestle, and it was close there for a moment. But it was the plasma ball, and not George, that broke to pieces. The Marsala Plasma shattered in George's hands, broke jaggedly into a hundred edged pieces, and clattered and crashed heavily on the stoney ground. And George was cut badly on the hands and forearms and chest by the jagged slivers of it.

George cursed, he howled with quick pain, he laughed at the crashing puzzle of it: the floating balloon that turned into jagged rock. And he laughed at the half dozen Oganta of both sexes who came with hasty bowls and cries of "Here, here, to me, to mine."

George shook and dribbled his running blood into the Ogantas' bowls. The big oafs loved the tang of blood, human blood or their own, in their strong stew. It was salt and condiment to them. And to George too. For he lept barefooted onto the shoulders of the chuckling Oganta girls and trod them. It was bloody revel.

"Here, here, to me, to mine," the earth girls also cried, partly in comedy, partly in novel passion. George Oneiron dribbled his blood into the crocks of Helen Damalis and Margaret Mondo and Bonta Chrysalis, and lept onto their shoulders also. Then, borne there by Margaret, he poured his blood into the common caldrons on the largest table.

George was bleeding a surprising quantity of blood from the cuts of the gas globule, that floating thing that had shattered so quickly into vitreous daggers that were heavier than stone or metal. The loss of blood made him light-headed and gave him the froggish passion. But he quickly received more blood. All the Oganta, then the other four of the earth people, slashed themselves with the dagger-shards of the broken globule and gave him their blood to drink. Now they were of one blood forever.

All five of the earth psychologists were quite young adults. This would give them closer and quicker understanding of the Oganta who were such vivid and outgoing oafs that even their dreams were on the outside. There was no denying that there was an abnormality about the Oganta, even beyond the differences of worlds and the differences of species.

The Oganta were a neotenic species who had lost, or almost lost, their adult form. As well as it can be explained in earth context, they were teen-agers forever whatever their age: and they seemed to age not at all after they had attained their high oafishness. There is no thing to which they might be compared in this: but imagine, if you dare, teen-ager attitudes and activities continued by certain individuals to a far greater age, twenty-two years, twenty-three, twenty-four, even further. If such things happened on earth where would earth be? Imagine neotenics breeding, reproducing, and never attaining an adult form. That was the state on Paravata.

The Oganta of Paravata were large. They looked like a cross between humans and frogs. They themselves said that they were analogous to the tadpoles who had been unable to make the frog leap. But to human earth eyes they looked like frogs and they leapt like frogs.

"But every frog is really a prince enchanted," Bonta Chrysalis said.

"I'd say that every prince is rather a frog in disguise," Philip Blax countered, "except that I'm sure it's been said before, and probably by me."

"Come here, Prince," Bonta Chrysalis cried suddenly, and one of the big Oganta lept into her arms and wrapped long froggy legs around her till Bonta herself could hardly be seen. But she'd made her choice. She'd taken one of the grinning gape-faced Oganta for her subject (subject for her study, and willing subject to her real whims) and she would not fail in this.

The Oganta were intelligent; or perhaps they only pretended to be, for a joke. They imbibed earth knowledge easily and literally, but they didn't take it too seriously. Their own culture was deliberately anti-intellectual, but they understood pretty well all that they rejected. They had an easy way with languages and lingos. They even had an easy way with the psychology texts that lay about there, fingering through them quickly, then burlesquing not only the words but also the ideas of them.

The Oganta also had (this is not fully understood, it is one of the mysteries that must be solved) that light way and that heavy way with weight.

The Oganta played one abominable instrument, the stringed hittur. But the five young earthlings did not find it as offensive as older earthlings would have. They knew that the whining tastelessness of it was an essential part of the Oganta. And they knew that even the vigorous Oganta could not be vigorous in everything. Even the hittur would be accepted, as one of the things that must be studied.

Helen Damalis had also acquired a boy friend, an oaf friend, a leaping frog friend, from among the Oganta there in the mountain inn. She hadn't done it as deftly or as regally as Bonta had taken hers. Perhaps it was that Helen was acquired by the Oganta. Helen wasn't regal, she wasn't strong, she wasn't much of anything at the moment. She looked like a very small sofa with a very large Oganta lounging on her.

The Oganta liked the earth folks. They slavered over them, they kissed them with great slurping sounds, they frog-leapt upon them. They insisted that the earth folks should play the leaping game also. This was the mystic game of leap-frog, the oldest game of the worlds. The leaping is always upon and not over, and the fun of the game is in going from weightlessness to staggering weight at just the wrong moment.

"We'll need neither notebooks nor recordings," Christopher Bullock was saying very solemnly (yet he was very unsolemnly a-romp and a-tromp on a playful and trollish female Oganta), "for the Marsala Plasma will serve for both. They are the crystal balls, crystal even in their gaseous state, and they record everything of the particular Oganta they attach to. We'll have everything down in the most solid recordings ever, petrified dream and person blobs."

There were five of these young psychologs from earth.

There was this Christopher Bullock: we will have to call him a young man of muscular mind; there's no other term that will serve. The playful and trollish female

Oganta had now picked Christopher up and draped him about her neck like a scarf: like a light scarf at first, then like a staggeringly heavy scarf. Christopher himself was learning a little about the light way and the heavy way with weight. There has always been something doubled about that name of Christopher, especially when it doubles into the name of Cristobal: there was once a man named Cristobal Colon (an old necromancer of Earth who doubled the Earth), though his name was regularized to Christopher Columbus. Though Christopher means Christ-Bearer, yet Cristobal is the phonetic equivalent of Crystal Ball and it has unchristly connotations. Just what is the real meaning of the crystal ball, and why was Christopher Bullock so interested in it?

The second of the young psychologs from earth was George Oneiron. George was a split person, and the two halves of him were stark idealism and total depravity. In each half George was a nice enough fellow, but the contrast within him was awkward. The halves of George were at the moment served by two female Oganta, one of them as spiritual, one of them as carnal as it is possible for neotenic frog-humans to be.

The third of the young psychologs from earth was Philip Blax. Philip had healed his own split and had become (in advance) a very little like one of the Oganta in appearance and attitude. Nothing special about Philip really.

But the fourth of the psychologs from earth was Bonta Chrysalis and she was something special. She was everything. She was magnificent in mind and body, splendid, soaring, regal, almost a flame. She was beauty and grace combined with power. She had always known the light way and the heavy way with things. The Oganta Frog, who might be the prince enchanted, had frog-lept onto her shoulder and perched there, and he was the largest of them all. But what is weight to a flame? And that big one, if he wasn't enchanted before, he was now, completely enchanted by Bonta.

And from Bonta Chrysalis we go to Helen Damalis who suffers by the comparison. Helen wasn't much. She had less substance than any of them, less even than Philip. Helen wasn't distinguished by the primary brain in her head or by the secondary spinal brain which all good psychologs must have. She hadn't beauty of face or grace of body, not by earth standards, not even by Paravata-Oganta standards. She was plastic, perhaps, and she might take the impression of these things, but she hadn't them of herself. She was an empty receptacle, an inelegant piece of pottery; yet she had a sullen intensity and an eagerness to be filled. She had a real hunger for life. One thing more: the Marsala Plasma, those gaseous blobs that were really crystal balls that could shatter into heavy fragments, followed and clung to Helen, as they did to all the Oganta, as they did not to the earth people. And Helen clung very closely to her Oganta boy friend, oaf friend, frog friend.

The fifth of the psychologs from earth was Margaret Mondo. She had an earthiness beyond any of them. This wasn't necessarily a roughness. Earth is more than that. It wasn't a lowness of any sort. Earth is much more than that. It was a primordial variety that she had, a many-rootedness. It was not true that Paravata was more earthy than earth; you knew that was not true when you looked at Margaret who was earth itself. She could contain them all, but nobody could contain her. So it wasn't an Oganta singling that she attracted, but a group, a trio of Oganta, two males and a female. She was too complex and vital to waste on a singling.

Ah, the young scientists had gathered up, or in some cases been gathered up by, their subjects. They went off with them now, riding them or ridden by them, in groups and tangles; off for study and for fun and for exploratory experience and for science.

The Oganta, so coarse and so open that they had their dreams on the outside.

And the five young mind-scientists from earth.

Five? Not six? Christopher, George, Philip, Bonta, Helen, Margaret. Do they not come to six?

No. There are five of them. Count them again carefully. See, there are five of them.

2

The crystal ball, it is everywhere phoney in its every form, and nowhere has it so many or such unusual forms as on Paravata. On Earth, as far back as one wants to go, to Babylon, to Chaldee, the crystal ball is in solid (though cloud-filled) form only, and it is the tool and scope of charlatans and oneiromancers. Even in those beginnings its users didn't understand its real form, and yet they preserved some slight pre-earth memory of its various phases. On Paravata, by accident, it has its full phases. It may be in gas or liquid or plastic or solid form; it may go from one to the other in a twinkling (the phrase was coined for that change in that thing).

But what can really be seen in any crystal ball? Futures? Yes, futures, pasts, presents, scenes, dreams, images, dramas, primary persons, secondary persons. The ball may go tricky and freeze forever any of these fleeting things. Very often it will seize a secondary person and freeze this person forever. That person, then, will never have had any existence except in the ball, it will never have been anything except petrified.

To say that the crystal ball is everywhere phoney is not to say that it is ineffectual. It is to say that it has misshapen or phoney effect. But it does have effect. It works, it works.

From the Notebooks of Christopher Bullock.
(Wasn't he the one who said they would need
neither notebooks nor recordings?)

Bonta Chrysalis and Margaret Mondo perhaps had the most success with their projects. Bonta's, it would turn out, would be a badly twisted success. Helen Damalis surely had the least success, though she believed she was having the greatest. She was realizing herself at least, she claimed. In a limited way that was true. Christopher Bullock may have had the most fun, what with that playful and trollish female Oganta of his, but even this is to be doubted. There was something unexpected to be found even in the troll. All the projects suffered in having no aim other than the mere study of the Oganta.

Could they be studied apart from their planet of Paravata? Were the Oganta isolated and discrete individuals? Were they interlinked groups with the personality residing in the groups? Were they mere fauna of their planet, a mobile grass of their world, manifestations, fungi? That was the trouble with the Oganta: they changed under the different points of view. As drops of water they were one thing; as small seas they were something quite opposite; as planetary oceans they might have a third and vastly different substance.

Philip Blax said that the Oganta themselves had no problems, that they were completely uninhibited and uncomplicated, that they were interchangeable modules of an unstructured society that knew neither anxiety nor doubt. Bonta said that in this Philip was wrong in a way unusual even for Philip. She said that the Oganta did have extreme anxieties, and that the better the intelligence and personality of the individual Oganta the greater was his anxiety. She said they had these anxieties because they had lost their adult form.

"It is well lost," Philip had said, "and I might wish that we could lose our own."

"You never had one and never will," Bonta told him. "I haven't my own completely yet, but I will have it. You are yourself like an Oganta, and it's yourself you see when you look at them. You're emptier than they are. You're not like the ones who are superior in intelligence and personality."

The plasma balls, the crystal balls, did make good notebooks and recorders; Christopher Bullock had been correct on that. The Oganta were such uninhibited (on the surface anyhow) and open creatures that they had their dreams on the outside of them: the psychologs from earth had said that from the beginning but without really understanding what they meant.

"The plasma ball is a bucket," Margaret Mondo said now. "It can become a bucketful of dreams, and it becomes heavier as it becomes fuller."

No need for other apparatus to study Oganta dreams. Allow a new and fresh Marsala Plasma to hover over an Oganta as he slept, either in the daytime or at night, and watch the plasma globe. The parade of dreams would be shown and sensed in that globe, vividly and colorfully, pungently and resoundingly. The Oganta dreamed better than they knew. Their dreams were more finely structured than their lives and had a greater diversity. They were real pageants, full of symbols and outright creations, enormous, overwhelming, spooky, powerful. Each superceded dream of the parade gathered itself like broken smoke and retreated into the center of the plasma to make way for more current presentations on the spherical stage nearest the surface. But all the dreams were recorded for all the senses and not one of them was lost.

George Oneiron made first discovery of a method of reconstructing the dissolved Oganta dreams. He'd affront a plasma ball that had been beside one of his Oganta subjects during her sleep period; he'd affront it and make it go heavy. He'd affront it still more and make it shatter into pieces. And each jagged broken fragment of it would display one of those bright jagged dreams. Turn one of those jagged fragments to another angle, and there was the same dream in another aspect, one that might have been completely missed at first viewing. George himself was very strong in the dreams of his two Oganta subjects, in a distorted form always, or in his two distorted forms.

Margaret Mondo said that George was doing it all wrong. She quickly discovered that there was no reason to affront the globes, still less reason to shatter them. There was no need to make them go heavy permanently; they received less well when they were always heavy. Let them go heavy and light, and heavy and light again. Margaret herself could resurrect out of the globes any dream or constellation of dreams by caressing them with her own magic hands. She could reconstruct them in sequence or out of sequence, any way she wished.

Having three Oganta subjects, Margaret sometimes used three globes. But she could make the three globes merge into one, and emerge out of it again. Sometimes there would then be four globes and not three: one composite globe, three discrete globes. Margaret was studying three individuals as well as one small nation.

After a while she maintained master globes. The individual globes, after each dream period, were merged with their master globes; and then they were emerged from them again, emptied and ready for reuse. There was no limit to the amount of data that a globe might hold.

Indexing and recovering the data were other matters. Margaret could effect these things with her magic hands. The others hadn't hands so magic as Margaret's, but they managed. Except Helen Damalis. She managed her material not at all; it managed her.

The Oganta needn't be sleeping to project these dream sequences. They projected always, when leaping or shouting, when slavering or loving, when guzzling or gorging, while wrestling or rolling, while rattling the air with their whining unmusic, while burlesquing and buffooning, while unstructuring themselves and their minds. Even their waking dreams were better than their waking lives. Why did the Oganta put themselves down so?

There was a certain pathos in the pageanted dreams of Christopher Bullock's subject, the playful and trollish Oganta girl. Oh, she was playful enough, cloud-shatteringly playful! Sequences taken from her playful dreams and reveries (reverie is the wrong word, it implies quietness and musing; there should be a word to express the whooping happy calamities and catastrophes of this alien girl) would later be enjoyed by a certain clientele of earth fellows in the manner of old stag movies. And she was trollish enough. She enjoyed her massive and misshapen burlesque of a body; it was the house she lived in. But there were other levels and aspects of the data that streamed and fountained up from this girl. There were odd caves and grottos in the mountain of her, some of them secluded and quite unexpected, rare ones, puzzling ones. It's a dull mountain that can labor (even trollishly) without bringing forth at least a small heap of gem-stones.

There was nobility in the interaction of Bonta Chrysalis and her enchanted Oganta subject. There was something cracked or usurping about that nobility though.

"But they do put it on a little thick," George Oneiron said correctly of them.

"Blunt as I am, I was never that blunt, or that empty," Philip Blax attacked them, and with justice.

"Oh, climb down from it, Bonta," Christopher mocked. "You'll get too high for your own head."

Even the ever kind and ever-magic Margaret Mondo wrung her hands and shook her head over the affair and said: "May I never be so pretentious as that! May God Himself never be! There are limits to things, and they pass the limit."

Helen Damalis perhaps said the strangest thing of all about the affair: "If they can make a thing like that come alive, is it helpless for myself? Air lives and turns into talking and walking crystal. Stones live, and float like air in air. Frogs live. Imaginary princes live. All I ever wanted was to live. Is there not magic enough for some of it to fall on me?"

Were they really so pretentious and outrageous, the things that Bonta and her charmed frog were attempting? This frog-Oganta had intimations and even expectations of adulthood now. Whether he had already had these intimations of himself or whether Bonta had given them to him is unknown, but he had them strongly.

There was now no more than one out of ten thousand Oganta who ever attained the old Rogha form, the old adult form. And these few who attained it were isolated in it, without mate or breed, and usually very old. All the other earth psychologs felt that this thing gone once should be gone forever. All the other Oganta felt that whatever state one should reach all should reach; that if they did break out of the top of themselves to a new state and development, it should not now be that old and lost state. There must have been something wrong with that old advanced state or it would never have been lost. Perhaps it was too pretentious in itself, and too contemptuous of its underlay.

It was strange that Bonta Chrysalis, that everything earthling girl, didn't understand this. Perhaps her own state was in her name and she was looking for a developed state for herself as well as for her subject. Perhaps, for all her easy attainments and brilliances, she herself was not adult and would not soon be.

It was strange that the enchanted Oganta himself, more intelligent and personable than the other Oganta, didn't realize that the old effective advanced form was now impossible. If attained now it would be mere sterility. On the word of the other Oganta of the immediate group, this one was the most gifted of them all. Why had he a faulty gift of vision in this?

Helen Damalis had the rockiest time of them all. She seemed, though, to be the most avid for the experience, even the very rocky experience. She had become attached to her subject, not he to her. And he was cruel to her with that offhanded and amazing cruelty of which only the Oganta are capable. He was a complete egotist and most of his dream sequences were parades and pageants of himself only, or himself against a dim background of other Oganta: other Oganta, and a flurry of inferior creatures which were not easy to identify. "Like a cross between an Oganta and a chicken." Was that more offensive than the earthlings' way of seeing the Oganta? "Like a cross between a human and a frog." It was Margaret who pointed out that this was the Oganta way (or this particular Oganta's way) of seeing the earth-humans.

But there had come another person and appearance into the dream sequence of this cruel Oganta now. This was the appearance of Helen Damalis herself. Oh, he dreamed of her! That was something. It was as if it made her real. What matter that she was only the secondary element in a shaggy form that was somewhat hermaphroditic and miscegenated? She was there. That was something.

George Oneiron projected his own split person onto his two subjects. It was all very brilliant in the tensions that it set up. George was making parades of his double self through the Oganta mediums. These were sculpted and directed dreams of himself and he loved them. Later viewers would love them also. They were good. They were excellent. But they weren't pure Oganta.

Margaret Mondo was wielding a small nation. To her own trio, two males and a female, she now added the boisterous, playful, trollish female of Christopher Bullock. And to herself she added Christopher: she'd always intended to do that. It might be that the development of the Oganta (Och, they *did* need development; it were catastrophe if they remained as they were for always) would come through these small but accreting nations of them. These were nuclei being created, some by the earthlings, some independent of them. The Oganta seemed the starkest individuals of any species anywhere, but it was only seeming. They began to accrete into these small nations now; and the personality was in the nations, not in the individuals. Happily this is not the case with many species: necessarily it was so with the Oganta. The small nation might be their new adult form.

The Oganta of Helen Damalis had broken all her bones and mangled her body almost beyond recognition. This pleased her: but it must not go as far as her extinction or all would be lost. She must hide, but she must maintain the relationship: so she must hide in the most obvious place of all. She attracted an empty Marsala Plasma and crept inside it. Then she merged it with the standing plasma globe, her Oganta's crystal ball of record. He would see her there mingled with himself; but he'd not know that this was her alive, so he'd not extinguish her to her death.

Bonta Chrysalis had just now (and most unfortunately) succeeded in her own experiment. She had disenchanted her frog. She had produced her prince. He stood now in his pride and royalty: he was an adult in the old line and form; he was a Rogha.

He was very proud. He was very old (the Oganta showed no ageing, whatever their years, but all the considerable years of this one were apparent in his new Rogha form). He was a royal Rogha, one of the elites, of the excellent ones. He was imposing in a way that neither Oganta nor human could ever be. He was extraordinary, he was magnificent, he was proud with the pride of the older angels. He was isolated. He was finished.

He was ridiculous. He was silly.

"I'm sorry," Bonta Chrysalis said lamely. She was still in bondage to her own state and youth. Chrysalis-dreams never accord with reality, but how could she have been so very wrong in this?

"Sorry?" the Rogha asked in regal voice. "You should be happy, small creature, in your limited way. You've been the instrument. You have restored me. Something has restored me. Now I have inherited to my rightful station, that of a natural and destined prince. I look around. I find that I am more than that. I see that it is very late in the day. All the kings are dead. Now I am the king."

In poetic justice, the oafish and unsensing Oganta almost deserved such an adult form. But they had lost it. There *is* a Providence.

The times had come to their end. These seminars, these field trips, cannot last for ever. It was time for the five earthlings to return to earth.

The Oganta, the new, small, but accreting nation of them, threw a bash for the five young psychologs from earth. It was rowdy, of course. It was loud almost beyond bearing. It was vulgar, it was boisterous, it was cacophonous with the whanging and whining of the stringed hitturs. It was at a mountain inn, one of those gape-wall places. It was just at frost-bite, and a light snow was sifting. The five youngish earth-folk were dressed near as barely as the Oganta.

Crudity, gluttony, guzzling and gorging. Tromping on tables and on torsos. Slurping and toothing from the common caldrons. The ancient and mystic game of leap-frog, and the wrestling and rolling of bodies.

But it was not quite the same sort of bash as the Oganta had thrown for them at their coming. Niceties had appeared. A new element was there, an element that you could hardly pin down with your two feet; but there was a difference. Come back in a thousand years and you'd be able to see the difference clearly.

The bash bashed on. Margaret and Christopher went to gather up the various records, the crystal balls (now solid and stoney, yet with clouds still drifting in them) that held the dream pageants and complexes of the curious small Oganta nation, and of their own curious human selves as seen through Oganta eyes.

George and Philip and Bonta came to them late in the day, bebashed and besotted, and the five earth psychologs were near packed for their return to earth.

"There is one missing," Margaret said. "I wonder if it is worth picking up? Oh, I'll do it. It'll be inferior, but it'll be different. Sometimes there are overlooked things to be found in artifacts that are inferior and different."

"Which?" Bonta asked.

"The crystal ball of record of the singling Oganta," Margaret said, "of the one unsociable Oganta who hated humans so much. But we persuaded him to let a recording ball accumulate on him. Oh, I bet it's full of hate! I'll get it."

Margaret Mondo got the crystal ball of record of the Oganta who hated humans. It was small, but heavy and weird. It wasn't entirely full of hate, not yet. There was one other slight element in it, not quite extinguished, outraged and terrified and squalling for attention.

"Margaret, get me out of here," the stone screeched. "I'm trapped in it, I tell you. I want to mend up my bones and go home to earth."

"My, aren't you an odd one," Margaret exclaimed. "What a dirty little masterpiece! He made you out of scraps of Bonta and myself, so how could he have made you so ugly?"

"Margaret, it's I, Helen Damalis! Get me out of here!"

"Why, how psychological of him! All the Oganta have an easy way with the lingos. He really named you that, did he, little hell heifer? Ah, what a shrilling little bad dream you are. One ugly clot of stone like this will show up the other globes in all their colorful beauty. Pack you away with the others, I will, and you'll be the comedy piece of the collection."

"Margaret, I'm Helen. Can't you understand? Run your magic hands over my globe and get me out of here. I'm Helen, the sixth one of the party."

"But we were always a party of five. Ah the look on you, it changes, it lowers, it explodes. There are stinking flames reeking about you, not dream clouds. More, dirty dream, more. Hate, hate, hate! Then I'll freeze you forever in the stone in your dull hatred. Oh, what a perfect little deformity you are!"

"Margaret, I hate you," the stone squalled, "I hate everybody. I'm alive, I tell you. I'm real. See me, hear me, smell me, get me out of here! I'm alive, I'm alive!"

"Yes, you're a lively little abomination, but never really alive. The worlds couldn't stand it if you were. More, uncreature, more, more if that's possible. Burn, scream, hate! That's it."

Then Margaret Mondo packed the little misshapen nightmare stone away with all the intricate and interesting crystal balls.

Go see it in the Oganta Collection. Really, it's the liveliest item of them all. Look at it there, wobble-eyed with horror and hatred, shrilling silently, pungent as brimstone, squalling against extinction, hating, outraged, absolutely petrified.

The Morning Rush or Happy Birthday, Dear Leah

LEE SAYE

THE PRE-MORNING Rush Traffic report came on and
Albert knew it was time to wake up. Not a bad morning,
he thought, hearing the comforting rush and whish of cars
going by on either side. He stretched before opening his
eyes and had his good mood spoiled by cracking his knee
on the dashboard. "Damn," said Albert. It was his first
word every morning since buying the new VW. Never had
he failed to hurt the same knee in the same manner.

"Not so loud, dear," said Mary. "The kids are still
asleep." How could she look so fresh after putting in a full
night at the wheel? Fresh, all right, thought Albert, but a
little tense this morning.

"How come you're still driving?" said Albert. "Hasn't
Leah taken the third shift since she got her Learner's
Permit?" Albert had already squirmed out of his pajamas

and was trying to thrash his way into his trousers. Buying the VW had been a great economy move, but a family of four really needed more room. Albert allowed the thought of a van to pass through his mind to be displaced as a limousine with shades drawn ghosted by in the next lane.

"I let her sleep," said Mary.

"Huh?" Albert came back to reality.

"I let Leah sleep because . . . because today's her birthday," said Mary. "Besides, it was such a nice night I just drove on through. I wanted to do a little thinking anyway. It's okay."

"Well, you gotta be tired," said Albert, pulling a blue bag from a slot under the dash, adjusting his trousers and slapping the bag into position. When he had finished he sealed the bag, shook it to activate the chemicals, and deposited it in the sump. "We're low on these, you know."

"Yes," said Mary. "We should hit the Milano Station before time for the Noon Rush, and we'll draw supplies there. If you're ready to take the wheel, I'll get your breakfast."

"Yeah, okay," said Albert, and with practiced moves they exchanged seats, Albert unusually aware of her thighs as she slid over him into the shotgun seat. Albert adjusted the air flow, turned out the headlights and settled into his seat.

"Whew," said Mary. "It feels good not to be driving. I guess I was tireder than I thought." She adjusted her skirt and lifted a battered plastic foam container from under her knees and opened it. "Not much left but chicken salad on whole wheat and tuna on white. Which do you want?"

"Neither. Just give me some coffee if there is any. How did we run out of food so fast?"

"Leah's birthday cake took up a lot of our ration when we passed the Berlin Station." Did her voice catch when she said that? "We'll have it early so it won't count against us at Milano." Mary took one of the vacuum bottles from

191 | *THE MORNING RUSH*

inside her door panel, sloshed it to make it heat, and poured Albert a cup.

Albert smiled his thanks, marveled at his wife's good looks, and took the cup. The day was shaping up pretty well. The sun was a red sphere hanging up there above the horizon in the haze, and Albert saw it glint off the endless car tops as he crossed an overpass. He drank the coffee and felt it open his gullet and splash warmly into his stomach. The Traffic Director's chopper rushed by overhead, and Albert checked his watch and heard the radio click automatically on again.

"Prepare to power down for the Morning Rush," said the Traffic Director's friendly voice. "Reduce speed to fifty kilometers per hour."

Albert jockeyed the VW up to the standard one meter from the Dodge station wagon he had been following for a month, set the hand throttle and released the accelerator. Mary was leaning over the seat shaking Marc, who grunted, snarled, blinked, rubbed his eyes, and wordlessly began squirming out of his pajamas.

"Don't wake up Leah," said Mary to Marc, handing him a blue bag. "We have to get ready for her birthday party. We'll see if Patti can come over if they're in the area."

"Aw," growled Marc, obviously not up to a day of big sister sissy talk. He used the blue bag, sealed and shook it weakly, and handed it to Mary who dropped it into the sump.

"Reduce speed to twenty kilometers per hour," said the radio, and Albert clicked the hand throttle down another notch. All over the 0700 time zone, which at the moment included parts of several continents, the motorcars slowed to a crawl.

Albert sat up with a start. In the tiny, grassy area between two intersecting expressways were three people! He had heard strange tales of land people all his life, and had even seen them from time to time, increasingly of late, in fact, but it always came as a surprise to see the scuzzy, unkempt vagabonds walking along the median or lounging about under a bridge, apparently unconcerned and obviously with no car to go to. And, thought Albert, strung out on all kinds of drugs, no doubt. Some were old, ragged, battered reprobates, but most were young and impertinent. Albert shook his head and gave silent thanks for an upbringing that had saved him from that. His father had been poor, but they had always had a decent car to live in, and anybody even mentioning the land people was asking for a clout.

"Look, Albert," said Mary, looking beautiful, refreshing, nervous, and holding a birthday cake with eleven candles all alight.

"Oh, yeah," said Albert. "Is she up?"

"She is now," said Leah, looking sleepy-eyed from the rear seat. "Birthday cake for breakfast?"

"Good morning and happy birthday," said Mary, handing the cake to Leah through the space between the seats. Leah blinked sleepily and looked at the cake in her lap. Mechanically she took the knife from her mess kit in her arm rest and started to cut.

"Blow out the candles first, dummy," said Marc. Leah looked up as though coming awake for the second time, blew out the candles and handed the cake back over the seat.

"Leah," said Mary, "we haven't sung Happy Birthday and you haven't made a wish or anything. . . ."

"Mom," said Leah, setting her jaw, "I don't want any. . . ."

"Here," said Albert, reaching behind his sunvisor and taking out a metal plate. "Here's what my girl wants, I'll bet. Her own Driver's License, all official and everything. I radioed for it when we came through Los Angeles. They transmitted it to us that early to be effective on this date because your Learner's record is so good, and it would have been six months before we passed another issue point." He handed the license between the seats, but no hand took it.

"I don't want a Driver's License, Father," said Leah.

"Reduce speed to five KPH," said the radio, and Albert almost rammed the Dodge station wagon before he got the VW slowed, his hand still holding the metal license over the seat. Uncertainly, he withdrew his hand, held it shoulder high beside him and looked at Mary. They crept to the crest of a rise and twenty solid lanes of five kilometer-per-hour Traffic stretched endlessly ahead, with the Rome Cutoff intersecting directly ahead, then the U-9471, and farther on, the Trans-Eurasian Transport Way.

"What does she, uh, mean?" said Albert.

Between the great highways were tiny patches of artificial grass or concrete, sometimes only a few square centimeters, sometimes as much as maybe forty square meters. And all around were the millions and billions of smoke-belching, honking motorcars, creeping along at five kilometers per hour—the depth of the Morning Rush. Albert saw a land person on one of the concrete islands, propped on a parcel of some sort picking his nose. Unusual, thought Albert, to see only one. They usually traveled in packs, for to be alone in their world, Albert thought, was tantamount to death.

"I mean I don't want a Driver's License, Father," said Leah so clearly that even a father could but comprehend. "I want to be a land person."

"Marc, connect your headphones to School Hookup," said Mary.

"Aw! I wanna hear this," he whined. Mary glared, and Marc plugged into the console on the back of the front seat, as ordered.

"What?" roared Albert. "A *land* person? No daughter of mine is gonna be no bum!"

"Increase speed," said the Traffic Director's voice. "Morning Rush is over." Albert caught a glimpse of the TD's chopper heading back to its perch atop the police Bus several hundred kilometers ahead. There were few revolving blue lights along the way and no stopped vehicles. It had been a good Morning Rush.

"I'm eleven years old today, Daddy," said Leah. "I can do whatever I want to now, and what I want is to be a *land* person, not a car person."

"Talk to your daughter, Mary," said Albert, flipping the toggle marked "legal" on the dash. "A. Gregg to Legal Unit. Advise as to legal status of eleven year old citizen."

"Independent," said the radio. "An eleven year old is of legal age."

"See there," said Leah.

"There's the Milano Station Matter Transmitter," said Marc, obviously not on his studies. It was lucky he spotted it anyway.

"Lord," said Mary, frantically tapping a telegraph key on her armrest. "I haven't even made a list. I'll just call for a standard order . . . the stuff we usually get. That'll have to hold us until Istanbul. Slow down Albert. We can't receive matter if we're out of line-of-sight."

Albert noted that Leah's announcement had excited him so that his speed was up over 150 KPH, and he let up abruptly.

"Get some peanut butter," whined Marc.

"Standby your gauges," said Mary as she finished sending. From the Milano Station Transmitter the supplies necessary to sustain the Gregg family were converted to energy and beamed out to be reconstituted in the VW's storage tanks.

"Fuel, one-hundred," said Albert, and Mary marked her pad.

"Food, one-hundred," said Leah.

"And general, ninety-eight," said Mary.

"What did they leave out?" said Marc.

"Nothing important, dear," said Mary. "They back-ordered the underpants I ordered Leah. They'll be ready when we get to Istanbul."

"Can you make it to Istanbul without your new drawers?" said Albert. "That's the next supply station."

"I'm not going through Istanbul, Father," said Leah. "I

am eleven years old; I want to be a land person; you can't stop me, so stop the car and let me out."

"Get *her*," said Albert. " 'Stop the car' she says. I never stopped a car in my life." Six lanes over a service chopper was changing a tire on a Fiat as it sped along at about fifty KPH.

"It's the same as slowing down, Father," said Marc, "but just keep pushing on the brake pedal."

"I know, I know, and shut up. Leah, what's with you? You're not serious about this land person thing are you? Just as you get big enough to help with the driving . . . and do you know how your mother and I would worry? Gees!"

"I want out, Father, so stop the car."

"No way. Forget it," said Albert, who then listened incredulously as Leah radioed the police. Albert and Mary exchanged glances.

"This is European Precinct Car Nine to Gregg VW. Acknowledge, please," said the radio.

"Gregg here," muttered Albert.

"Look, mister, we sympathize one-hundred, but the kid's right. You gotta let her out," said the radio. "Now follow my instructions and you should be all right. Ever stopped a car before?"

"No," said Albert.

"Doesn't matter," said the radio. "Work your way over to the right-hand lane."

"But I've been in Lane Four for six years," said Albert. "I don't like to change lanes." Why must a man be asked to do so many things at once that he is unprepared to do, that he never thought he would have to do?

"Move on over, Mister Gregg."

Albert craned his neck and squinted through the tiny rear window, waited for a Mercedes to pass, then darted over two lanes causing a pick-up truck to slow violently and a bead of sweat to pop out at the base of Albert's skull. "Little rusty," said Albert. Mary patted his hand. Albert used the mirror the next time and found himself safe and sound in the curb lane.

"Pull off onto the apron," said the radio, and Albert, like a robot now, bumped the VW over the low curb and up onto the narrow emergency apron. "Apply brakes," said the radio. "More . . . more . . . just like reducing speed for Morning Rush, isn't it? . . . more . . . more . . ."

Albert's fists were tight about the steering wheel and the back of his head throbbed with tension.

"Engage the clutch," said the radio. "Now, more brakes . . . more brakes . . . more . . . that's it . . . that's it . . . a little more . . . and you've got it!"

Albert closed his eyes and stood up on the brake pedal and for the first time in his life the only motion Albert Gregg had was that he shared with the planet as it carved its tunnel through space. Before Albert could deal with this new sensation Leah was through the sun-roof, the one luxury they had permitted themselves on the new car, and Mary said "Look," as their daughter stumbled away as fast as she could on legs that had never walked but on the family exerciser.

"Goddamn," said Albert. "My little girl, my Leah."

"Aw, we'll have more room without her," said Marc, somewhere between ecstasy and tears.

Mary said nothing, but put a fist to the corner of her mouth and stared out the side window and a circuit was somewhere closed that told Albert that Mary had known all along. The whispered mother-daughter talks half heard during Albert's turn to sleep, and Mary had let Leah sleep rather than take her shift at the wheel. . . . Albert looked out in the direction Leah had taken but saw only a few feet of cement with oil stains, litter, and a crusty sprig of grass. Beyond that was the roaring, moving wall of cars and vans and cab-overs and semis and wreckers and pick-ups of every make or model or size or year or condition.

"Move it, VW," said the voice of the Traffic Director on the radio.

"Huh?" said Albert. "Oh, yes." He had never started from a standing stop before, but Traffic was slowing down to look at him, so he awkwardly dropped the clutch and jerked out into the curb lane, activated his signal and headed for Lane Four. It felt good to go through the gears, to match speeds with the living, moving world of the road, and to take one's proper place in the cosmic scheme of things. A land person, long-haired and dirty, skipped nimbly in front of the VW and Albert slowed briefly, a courtesy he had never before extended. Somewhere on a filthy piece of dirt was Leah, maybe alone, maybe already with a pack of the jackal-like land people. Eleven years old.

"Can I watch television instead of plugging in School Hookup for the rest of the day, Mom?" said Marc.

"Yes, Marc, you may."

You're too damned permissive, thought Albert. Just look how Leah turned out. But Albert couldn't find a voice to say it.

"I gave her an emergency re-call device," said Mary. "She can call us if she needs us."

"Yeah," said Albert, forcing words around an obstruction in his throat. "She'll activate it in Milano, and we'll be through Caracas. Besides, she'll throw it away or somebody will take it off her to decoy suckers into traps. Forget her. She's gone."

"Reduce speed to ten kilometers per hour," said the radio. Time for Noon Rush already? Albert released the accelerator and clicked down the hand throttle. Overhead a chopper was delivering a new car, a Buick, to a new owner on an adjacent freeway, and eight lanes over a cigar pennant on the antenna of a Ford signaled the birth of a baby.

"I need to use the blue bag, Mommy," said Marc. Mary handed the device over the back of the seat. "Boy, do I have a lot of room back here without old Leah. Boy, this is great!" Marc used the bag, sealed and shook it, then handed it back to his mother.

"Appropriate," said Albert, aloud.